Acclaim for Madeleine Thien's

simple recipes

"*Simple Recipes* introduces a writer of precocious poise.... The austere grace and polished assurance of Thien's prose are remarkable.... She has a way with the small, quiet image that sums up an inexpressible ache.... Her stories are peopled by fractured families; her characters are suffused with a kind of bewildered longing for domestic harmony.... The trajectories of Thien's stories are unpredictable; though her characters dream of following simple recipes, they are themselves undeniably original creations."　　— Janice P. Nimura, *New York Times Book Review*

"A sense of longing, and then of rupture, characterizes these delicate stories from a thrillingly gifted new writer. I hope we will hear a great deal more from Madeleine Thien."
　　— Anita Shreve, author of *The Pilot's Wife* and *Sea Glass*

"Excellent and wrenching.... Thien's first collection exhibits a very Alice Munro–like combination of delicacy and gravity.... In graceful counterbalance to the restraint of her prose, Thien's portraits of these painful, guilt-ridden, love-drenched relationships are remarkably rich."　　— Donna Rifkind, *Baltimore Sun*

"A fine collection.... Thien shows a rare, measured, and perceptive understanding.... Families, we are often told, are the basic building block of society. Rarely is the subject treated with the wisdom and open-eyed compassion that Thien displays here."
　　— Martin Wallace, *National Post*

"The stoic Canadian women who narrate Thien's graceful stories of working-class families gone awry have a way of quietly bringing the reader face to face with astonishing moments of parental cruelty, neglect, or, worst of all, indifference. It's as if these women have no reason not to be heartbreakingly low-key about childhoods spent in foster care, dealing with flaky moms, or warding off sexual abuse. . . . Her delicate prose turns out to be surprisingly resilient, holding these weighty familial betrayals aloft as if it were a luminous safety net."
— Mark Rozzo, *Los Angeles Times*

"A dazzling debut. . . . The young women in *Simple Recipes* find their homes shaken by cultural and generational differences. . . . A reminder that home is not always necessarily where the heart is."
— Megan O'Grady and Valerie Steiker, *Vogue*

"At 27, this promising young writer demonstrates a knack for characterization that makes the buzz surrounding her spare, rhapsodic prose understandable — and well deserved."
— Mimi Kriegsman, *Time Out New York*

"A polished, remarkable debut. . . . Thien's stories unfold with the complexity of life, rather than the predictability of fiction. . . . A tour de force of storytelling."
— Robert J. Wiersema, *Vancouver Sun*

"Richly layered stories. . . . A lovely, composed sorrowfulness pervades Thien's delicate yet powerful debut. Her characters, each struggling with a burden of love, fear, and guilt, revisit their pasts looking for clues that might free their present selves."
— Sarah Gianelli, *Portland Oregonian*

"Thien's wistful stories are universal explorations of family and yearning. . . . Their strength lies in the way she captures the distorted perspective of childhood and the confusion that accompanies the coming of age."   — Robert Weibezahl, *Bookpage*

"Powerful. . . . A graceful debut collection. . . . The simplicity of Thien's narration belies the complexity of her themes. She is a writer to watch." — *Publishers Weekly*

"A deft and mesmerizing feat. . . . Thien writes clearly and sparingly about all the muddy complexities of human connection; her words are so perfect and transparent that everything behind them is visible. They are like the whisper that stills a busy room." — Jeanie MacFarlane, *Toronto Star*

"In finely crafted, crystal-clear prose, Thien demonstrates what it is to face loss. . . . We come away with a wiser understanding of 'the human condition.' Could more be asked of an author?" — Bill Robinson, *MostlyFiction.com*

"Thien's writing is sparse and clean and often works on many levels. When she describes a father's ritual of washing and cooking rice you know there is a life lesson there. These stories are heartbreaking." — Ginny Merdes, *Seattle Post-Intelligencer*

"Seven spare, eloquent tales of family ties that fray but don't break. . . . Rich in detail, with memory serving to acknowledge complexity and to preserve what would otherwise be lost. . . . Truthful and suffused with quiet ache: a welcome collection." — *Kirkus Reviews*

"Thien joins the proud Canadian tradition led by Alice Munro, mining the territory of family dynamics and legacies with bold awareness and poetic delicacy. Parents and children, men and women, move toward and away from one another as they weather the various dysfunctions and heartbreaks of life, and then slowly, over time, turn guilt or anger into understanding, even acceptance. . . . These wise and richly wrought stories are a gem of a read." — Beth Taylor, *Providence Journal*

simple

recipes

simple

recipes

stories *for Christine, with love,*

MADELEINE THIEN

Madeline T C

BACK BAY BOOKS

Little, Brown and Company
Boston   New York   London

Originally published in hardcover by Little, Brown and Company,
June 2002
First Back Bay paperback edition, June 2003

The characters and events in this book are fictitious. Any similarity to
real persons, living or dead, is coincidental and not intended by the
author.

First published in Canada by McClelland and Stewart in 2001.

The epigraph on page vii is taken from *Water Memory* by Roo Borson
(Toronto: McClelland & Stewart Ltd.). Copyright © 1996 by Roo
Borson. Reprinted by permission of the publisher. The conversation
with Madeleine Thien reprinted in the reading group guide first
appeared at www.FictionAddiction.net, copyright © 2002.

Library of Congress Cataloging-in-Publication Data
Thien, Madeleine.
    Simple recipes : stories / by Madeleine Thien. — 1st U.S. ed.
        p. cm.
    Contents: Simple recipes — Four days from Oregon —
Alchemy — Dispatch — House — Bullet train — A map of the city.
    ISBN 0-316-83316-9 (hc) / 0-316-16869-6 (pb)
    1. Canada — Social life and customs — Fiction. 2. Conflict of
generations — Fiction. I. Title.
PR9199.3.T447 S5 2002
813'.6 — dc21   2001050475

10 9 8 7 6 5 4 3 2 1

Q-FF

Printed in the United States of America

This book is for my family, with love.

A house is a simple construct.
The builders die, but it goes on.
And still every childhood matters,
like mint grown in the shade,
all translation is painstaking,
and has no natural melody.
The world may be old,
but even then it was old,
without end or beginning.

— Roo Borson,
from "Milk"

contents

Simple Recipes / 1

Four Days from Oregon / 21

Alchemy / 55

Dispatch / 77

House / 99

Bullet Train / 127

A Map of the City / 159

Acknowledgments / 229

Simple Recipes

There is a simple recipe for making rice. My father taught it to me when I was a child. Back then, I used to sit up on the kitchen counter watching him, how he sifted the grains in his hands, sure and quick, removing pieces of dirt or sand, tiny imperfections. He swirled his hands through the water and it turned cloudy. When he scrubbed the grains clean, the sound was as big as a field of insects. Over and over, my father rinsed the rice, drained the water, then filled the pot again.

The instructions are simple. Once the washing is done, you measure the water this way — by resting the tip of your index finger on the surface of the rice. The water should reach the bend of your first knuckle.

My father did not need instructions or measuring cups. He closed his eyes and felt for the waterline.

Sometimes I still dream my father, his bare feet flat against the floor, standing in the middle of the kitchen. He wears old buttoned shirts and faded sweatpants drawn at the waist. Surrounded by the gloss of the kitchen counters, the sharp angles of the stove, the fridge, the shiny sink, he looks out of place. This memory of him is so strong, sometimes it stuns me, the detail with which I can see it.

Every night before dinner, my father would perform this ritual – rinsing and draining, then setting the pot in the cooker. When I was older, he passed this task on to me but I never did it with the same care. I went through the motions, splashing the water around, jabbing my finger down to measure the water level. Some nights the rice was a mushy gruel. I worried that I could not do so simple a task right. "Sorry," I would say to the table, my voice soft and embarrassed. In answer, my father would keep eating, pushing the rice into his mouth as if he never expected anything different, as if he noticed no difference between what he did so well and I so poorly. He would eat every last mouthful, his chopsticks walking quickly across the plate. Then he would rise, whistling, and clear the table, every motion so clean and sure, I would be convinced by him that all was well in the world.

¤

My father is standing in the middle of the kitchen. In his right hand he holds a plastic bag filled with water. Caught inside the bag is a live fish.

The fish is barely breathing, though its mouth opens and closes. I reach up and touch it through the plastic bag, trailing my fingers along the gills, the soft, muscled body, pushing my finger overtop the eyeball. The fish looks straight at me, flopping sluggishly from side to side.

My father fills the kitchen sink. In one swift motion he overturns the bag and the fish comes sailing out with the water. It curls and jumps. We watch it closely, me on my tiptoes, chin propped up on the counter. The fish is the length of my arm from wrist to elbow. It floats in place, brushing up against the sides of the sink.

I keep watch over the fish while my father begins the preparations for dinner. The fish folds its body, trying to turn or swim, the water nudging overtop. Though I ripple tiny circles around it with my fingers, the fish stays still, bobbing side to side in the cold water.

For many hours at a time, it was just the two of us. While my mother worked and my older brother played outside, my father and I sat on the couch, flipping channels. He loved cooking shows. We watched *Wok with Yan,* my father passing judgement on Yan's methods. I was enthralled when Yan transformed orange peels into swans. My father sniffed. "I can do that," he said. "You don't have to be a genius to do that." He placed a sprig of green onion in water and showed me how it bloomed like a flower. "I know many tricks like this," he said. "Much more than Yan."

Still, my father made careful notes when Yan demonstrated Peking Duck. He chuckled heartily at Yan's punning. "Take a wok on the wild side!" Yan said, pointing his spatula at the camera.

"Ha ha!" my father laughed, his shoulders shaking. "*Wok* on the wild side!"

In the mornings, my father took me to school. At three o'clock, when we came home again, I would rattle off everything I learned that day. "The brachiosaurus," I informed him, "eats only soft vegetables."

My father nodded. "That is like me. Let me see your forehead." We stopped and faced each other in the road. "You have a high forehead," he said, leaning down to take a closer look. "All smart people do."

I walked proudly, stretching my legs to match his steps. I was overjoyed when my feet kept time with his, right, then left, then right, and we walked like a single unit. My father was the man of tricks, who sat for an hour mining a watermelon with a circular spoon, who carved the rind into a castle.

My father was born in Malaysia and he and my mother immigrated to Canada several years before I was born, first settling in Montreal, then finally in Vancouver. While I was born into the persistence of the Vancouver rain, my father was born in the wash of a monsoon country. When I was young, my parents tried to teach me their language but it never came easily to me. My father ran his thumb gently over my mouth, his face kind, as if trying to see what it was that made me different.

My brother was born in Malaysia but when he immigrated with my parents to Canada the language left him. Or he forgot it, or he refused it, which is also common, and this made my father angry. "How can a child forget a language?" he would ask my mother. "It is because the child is lazy. Because the child chooses not to remember." When he was twelve years old, my brother stayed away in the afternoons. He drummed the soccer ball up and down the back alley, returning home only at dinner time. During the day, my mother worked as a sales clerk at the Woodward's store downtown, in the building with the red revolving W on top.

In our house, the ceilings were yellowed with grease. Even the air was heavy with it. I remember that

I loved the weight of it, the air that was dense with the smell of countless meals cooked in a tiny kitchen, all those good smells jostling for space.

The fish in the sink is dying slowly. It has a glossy sheen to it, as if its skin is made of shining minerals. I want to prod it with both hands, its body tense against the pressure of my fingers. If I hold it tightly, I imagine I will be able to feel its fluttering heart. Instead, I lock eyes with the fish. *You're feeling verrrry sleepy*, I tell it. *You're getting verrrry tired.*

Beside me, my father chops green onions quickly. He uses a cleaver that he says is older than I am by many years. The blade of the knife rolls forward and backward, loops of green onion gathering in a pyramid beside my father's wrist. When he is done, he rolls his sleeve back from his right hand, reaches in through the water, and pulls the plug.

The fish in the sink floats and we watch it in silence. The water level falls beneath its gills, beneath its belly. It drains and leaves the sink dry. The fish is lying on its side, mouth open and its body heaving. It leaps sideways and hits the sink. Then up again. It curls and snaps, lunging for its own tail. The fish sails into the air, dropping hard. It twitches violently.

My father reaches in with his bare hands. He lifts the fish out by the tail and lays it gently on the counter.

While holding it steady with one hand, he hits the head with the flat of the cleaver. The fish falls still, and he begins to clean it.

¤

In my apartment, I keep the walls scrubbed clean. I open the windows and turn the fan on whenever I prepare a meal. My father bought me a rice cooker when I first moved into my own apartment, but I use it so rarely it stays in the back of the cupboard, the cord wrapped neatly around its belly. I have no longing for the meals themselves, but I miss the way we sat down together, our bodies leaning hungrily forward while my father, the magician, unveiled plate after plate. We laughed and ate, white steam fogging my mother's glasses until she had to take them off and lay them on the table. Eyes closed, she would eat, crunchy vegetables gripped in her chopsticks, the most vivid green.

¤

My brother comes into the kitchen and his body is covered with dirt. He leaves a thin trail of it behind as he walks. The soccer ball, muddy from outside, is encircled in one arm. Brushing past my father, his face is tense.

Beside me, my mother sprinkles garlic onto the fish. She lets me slide one hand underneath the fish's head, cradling it, then bending it backwards so that she can fill the fish's insides with ginger. Very carefully, I turn the fish over. It is firm and slippery, and beaded with tiny, sharp scales.

At the stove, my father picks up an old teapot. It is full of oil and he pours the oil into the wok. It falls in a thin ribbon. After a moment, when the oil begins crackling, he lifts the fish up and drops it down into the wok. He adds water and the smoke billows up. The sound of the fish frying is like tires on gravel, a sound so loud it drowns out all other noises. Then my father steps out from the smoke. "Spoon out the rice," he says as he lifts me down from the counter.

My brother comes back into the room, his hands muddy and his knees the color of dusty brick. His soccer shorts flutter against the backs of his legs. Sitting down, he makes an angry face. My father ignores him.

Inside the cooker, the rice is flat like a pie. I push the spoon in, turning the rice over, and the steam shoots up in a hot mist and condenses on my skin. While my father moves his arms delicately over the stove, I begin dishing the rice out: first for my father, then my mother, then my brother, then myself. Behind me the fish is cooking quickly. In a crockery pot, my father steams cauliflower, stirring it round and round.

My brother kicks at a table leg.

"What's the matter?" my father asks.

He is quiet for a moment, then he says, "Why do we have to eat fish?"

"You don't like it?"

My brother crosses his arms against his chest. I see the dirt lining his arms, dark and hardened. I imagine chipping it off his body with a small spoon.

"I don't like the eyeball there. It looks sick."

My mother tuts. Her nametag is still clipped to her blouse. It says *Woodward's,* and then, *Sales Clerk.* "Enough," she says, hanging her purse on the back of the chair. "Go wash your hands and get ready for supper."

My brother glares, just for a moment. Then he begins picking at the dirt on his arms. I bring plates of rice to the table. The dirt flies off his skin, speckling the tablecloth. "Stop it," I say crossly.

"*Stop it,*" he says, mimicking me.

"Hey!" My father hits his spoon against the counter. It *pings,* high-pitched. He points at my brother. "No fighting in this house."

My brother looks at the floor, mumbles something, and then shuffles away from the table. As he moves farther away, he begins to stamp his feet.

Shaking her head, my mother takes her jacket off. It slides from her shoulders. She says something to my father in the language I can't understand. He merely shrugs his shoulders. And then he replies, and I think his words are so familiar, as if they are words I should know, as if maybe I did know them once but then I forgot them. The language that they speak is full of soft vowels, words running together so that I can't make out the gaps where they pause for breath.

My mother told me once about guilt. Her own guilt she held in the palm of her hands, like an offering. But your guilt is different, she said. You do not need to hold on to it. Imagine this, she said, her hands running along my forehead, then up into my hair. Imagine, she said. Picture it, and what do you see?

A bruise on the skin, wide and black.

A bruise, she said. Concentrate on it. Right now, it's a bruise. But if you concentrate, you can shrink it, compress it to the size of a pinpoint. And then, if you want to, if you see it, you can blow it off your body like a speck of dirt.

She moved her hands along my forehead.

I tried to picture what she said. I pictured blowing it away like so much nothing, just these little pieces that didn't mean anything, this complicity that I could magically walk away from. She made me believe in the strength of my own thoughts, as if I could make appear what had never existed. Or turn it around. Flip it over so many times you just lose sight of it, you lose the tail end and the whole thing disappears into smoke.

My father pushes at the fish with the edge of his spoon. Underneath, the meat is white and the juice runs down along the side. He lifts a piece and lowers it carefully onto my plate.

Once more, his spoon breaks skin. Gingerly, my father lifts another piece and moves it towards my brother.

"I don't want it," my brother says.

My father's hand wavers. "Try it," he says, smiling. "Take a wok on the wild side."

"No."

My father sighs and places the piece on my mother's plate. We eat in silence, scraping our spoons across the dishes. My parents use chopsticks, lifting their bowls and motioning the food into their mouths. The smell of food fills the room.

Savoring each mouthful, my father eats slowly, head tuned to the flavors in his mouth. My mother takes her glasses off, the lenses fogged, and lays them on the table. She eats with her head bowed down, as if in prayer.

Lifting a stem of cauliflower to his lips, my brother sighs deeply. He chews, and then his face changes. I have a sudden picture of him drowning, his hair waving like grass. He coughs, spitting the mouthful back onto his plate. Another cough. He reaches for his throat, choking.

My father slams his chopsticks down on the table. In a single movement, he reaches across, grabbing my brother by the shoulder. "I have tried," he is saying. "I don't know what kind of son you are. To be so ungrateful." His other hand sweeps by me and bruises into my brother's face.

My mother flinches. My brother's face is red and his mouth is open. His eyes are wet.

Still coughing, he grabs a fork, tines aimed at my father, and then in an unthinking moment, he heaves it at him. It strikes my father in the chest and drops.

"I hate you! You're just an asshole, you're just a fucking asshole chink!" My brother holds his plate in his hands. He smashes it down and his food scatters across the table. He is coughing and spitting. "I wish you weren't my father! I wish you were dead."

My father's hand falls again. This time pounding downwards. I close my eyes. All I can hear is someone screaming. There is a loud voice. I stand awkwardly, my hands covering my eyes.

"Go to your room," my father says, his voice shaking.

And I think he is talking to me so I remove my hands.

But he is looking at my brother. And my brother is looking at him, his small chest heaving.

A few minutes later, my mother begins clearing the table, face weary as she scrapes the dishes one by one over the garbage.

I move away from my chair, past my mother, onto the carpet, and up the stairs.

Outside my brother's bedroom, I crouch against the wall. When I step forward and look, I see my father holding the bamboo pole between his hands. The pole is smooth. The long grains, fine as hair, are pulled together, at intervals, jointed. My brother is lying on the floor, as if thrown down and dragged there. My father raises the pole into the air.

I want to cry out. I want to move into the room between them, but I can't.

It is like a tree falling, beginning to move, a slow arc through the air.

The bamboo drops silently. It rips the skin on my brother's back. I cannot hear any sound. A line of blood edges quickly across his body.

The pole rises and again comes down. I am afraid of bones breaking.

My father lifts his arms once more.

On the floor, my brother cries into the carpet, pawing at the ground. His knees folded into his chest, the crown of his head burrowing down. His back is hunched over and I can see his spine, little bumps on his skin.

The bamboo smashes into bone and the scene in my mind bursts into a million white pieces.

My mother picks me up off the floor, pulling me across the hall, into my bedroom, into bed. Everything is wet, the sheets, my hands, her body, my face, and she soothes me with words I cannot understand because all I can hear is screaming. She rubs her cool hands against my forehead. "Stop," she says. "Please stop," but I feel loose, deranged, as if everything in the known world is ending right here.

In the morning, I wake up to the sound of oil in the pan and the smell of French toast. I can hear my mother bustling around, putting dishes in the cupboards.

No one says anything when my brother doesn't come down for breakfast. My father piles French toast and syrup onto a plate and my mother pours a glass of milk. She takes everything upstairs to my brother's bedroom.

As always, I follow my father around the kitchen. I track his footprints, follow behind him and hide in the shadow of his body. Every so often, he reaches down and ruffles my hair with his hands. We cast a spell, I think. The way we move in circles, how he cooks without thinking because this is the task that comes to him effortlessly. He smiles down at me, but when he does this, it somehow breaks the spell. My father stands in place, hands dropping to his sides as if he has forgotten what he was doing mid-motion. On the walls, the paint is peeling and the floor, unswept in days, leaves little pieces of dirt stuck to our feet.

My persistence, I think, my unadulterated love, confuse him. With each passing day, he knows I will find it harder to ignore what I can't comprehend, that I will be unable to separate one part of him from another. The unconditional quality of my love for him will not last forever, just as my brother's did not. My father stands in the middle of the kitchen, unsure. Eventually, my mother comes downstairs again and puts her arms around him and holds him, whispering something to him, words that to me are meaningless and incomprehensible. But she offers them to him, sound after sound, in a language that was stolen from some other place, until he drops his head and remembers where he is.

Later on, I lean against the door frame upstairs and listen to the sound of a metal fork scraping against a dish. My mother is already there, her voice rising and falling. She is moving the fork across the plate, offering my brother pieces of French toast.

I move towards the bed, the carpet scratchy, until I can touch the wooden bed-frame with my hands.

My mother is seated there, and I go to her, reaching my fingers out to the buttons on her cuff and twisting them over to catch the light.

"Are you eating?" I ask my brother.

He starts to cry. I look at him, his face half hidden in the blankets.

"Try and eat," my mother says softly.

He only cries harder but there isn't any sound. The pattern of sunlight on his blanket moves with his body. His hair is pasted down with sweat and his head moves forward and backward like an old man's.

At some point I know my father is standing at the entrance of the room but I cannot turn to look at him. I want to stay where I am, facing the wall. I'm afraid that if I turn around and go to him, I will be complicit, accepting a portion of guilt, no matter how small that piece. I do not know how to prevent this from happening again, though now I know, in the end, it will break us apart. This violence will turn all my love to shame and grief. So I stand there, not looking at him or my brother. Even my father, the magician, who can make something beautiful out of nothing, he just stands and watches.

A face changes over time, it becomes clearer. In my father's face, I have seen everything pass. Anger that has stripped it of anything recognizable, so that it is only a face of bones and skin. And then, at other times, so much pain that it is unbearable, his face so full of grief it might dissolve. How to reconcile all that I know of him and still love him? For a long time, I thought it was not possible. When I was a child, I did not love my father because he was complicated, because he was human, because he needed me to. A child does not know yet how to love a person that way.

How simple it should be. Warm water running over, the feel of the grains between my hands, the sound of it like stones running along the pavement. My father would rinse the rice over and over, sifting it between his fingertips, searching for the impurities, pulling them out. A speck, barely visible, resting on the tip of his finger.

If there were some recourse, I would take it. A cupful of grains in my open hand, a smoothing out, finding the impurities, then removing them piece by piece. And then, to be satisfied with what remains.

Somewhere in my memory, a fish in the sink is dying slowly. My father and I watch as the water runs down.

Four Days from Oregon

I

Once, in the middle of the night, our mother Irene sat on our bed and listed off the ways she was unhappy. She looked out the window and stroked our hair and sometimes she lapsed into silence, as if even she didn't know the full extent of it, where to finish, when to hold back. And all the things that made her unhappy were mixed in with things that made her happy, too, like this house. It was full to the brim. Sometimes, she said, she sat in the bathroom because it was the smallest room with a door that locked. But even then she could hear us, me and my sisters Helen and Joanne, and our father, all of us creaking the floorboards and talking over the television and filling the quiet. Hearing us pulled her out every time. She would come out of the bathroom and track us down. She said she wanted to tuck us under her arm like a rolled-up paper and run away.

We were just kids then — Helen was nine, Joanne was seven, and I was six — but we thought of our mother as a young girl. She cried so much and had a temper. She joked about running off on her thirtieth birthday. "Almost there," she told us, joking. "Better pack your bags."

When our mother was unhappy, she broke things. She slammed the kitchen door over and over until its window crumpled and shattered to the floor. In our bare feet, we tiptoed around the pieces. Our father ignored it. He said, "Tell your crazy mother there's a phone call for her." He said *crazy* with a funny look in his eye, like he didn't really believe it. But we saw it ourselves, the plates flying from her hands, her face empty. Our father turned away and left the house. He walked slowly down the alley.

Only once did Irene leave us. We waited for her tirelessly. In the middle of the night, in our bed wider than a boat, we listened for her car on the road. We fought sleep, but she didn't come that night or the next. While she was gone, our father sat at the kitchen table like an old man. Already his hair had tufts of gray and his skin hung loose around his mouth and eyes. "Like a dog," he said, running his hands over his head. "Don't I look just like a dog?"

My sisters and I rode our bikes up and down the alley. When we were winded, we played in the garage, climbing up onto the roof of our father's brown Malibu. He poked his head in, said, "What's this, now?"

"Tea party," Helen told him, though we weren't really doing anything.

He nodded. "You like it better in the garage than in the house. It's your mother. There's something wrong in her head."

One day after school, she was back on the couch, her fingers ragged from worry. "I missed you," she said, pulling us in. My sisters and I sat on top of her body. We held her arms and legs down while she laughed, struggling to sit up.

Sometimes Irene was well and she put on the *Nutcracker Suite*, twirling us around the room. At times like this, she would embrace our father. She would kiss his face, his eyebrows and mouth. They waltzed around the living room. She kept stepping on his feet. He shrugged. "It's not the end of the world," he said.

Our mother shook her head. "No," she told him, "it never is."

The first time Tom came by, he shook our hands. He said, "So you're the Terrible Threesome," winking at us. Irene told us he was someone she worked with in the department store. He worked in Sports and Leisure. The second time he came, he brought three badminton rackets and a container full of plastic birdies. He and Irene sat on the steps drinking pink-tinted coolers. We batted the rackets through the air, knocking the birdies from one side of the lawn to the other. Joanne, always moody, aimed one through the tire swing. Another cleared the fence and landed in the neighbor's yard.

"Can't you hit straight?" Helen said, impatient.

Tom stood up on the balcony, waving his arms in the air. "I can bring some more tomorrow!"

Joanne turned her back on him and whipped one into the hedge.

Afterwards, Helen pocketed the last remaining birdie and we went down to the storage area beneath the porch. We planted the birdie in a cinder block, covered it with mud, then left it to bake in the after-noon sun. Through the floorboards we could hear Irene's voice, shy and laughing, and the long silences that came and went all afternoon, interrupted by the creaky sound of the screen door swinging shut. We watched Tom drive away, his hand stretching out of the car window, waving back to us.

Our father came home at six o'clock. Helen told him the screen door needed oiling again and he took us out back, oil on his hands. He rubbed the oil along the metal spoke so that when he threw the door open again it closed slow as ever, but without a sound on the wind, just the quiet click of the latch closing.

My sisters and I sat outside with him, our bare legs dangling between the porch steps. Our father pulled a photograph from his pocket. He'd come across it at the office, he explained, a picture of Main Street from a hundred years ago. In the photograph, there were no cars, just wide streets but no concrete, dirt piled down, women in long dresses, their hems bringing up the dust. I told my father I couldn't imagine streets without cars, trolleys and everything, horses idling on the corners. He said, "It's progress, you see, and it comes whether you welcome it or not."

Our father laid the photograph down. He said he could stand on the back steps and stare out until the yard fell away. He could see the house where he grew up, plain as day. It was in another country, and he remembered fields layered into the hillside. A person could grow anything there — tea, rice, coffee beans. I would always remember this because he had never talked about these things before. When he was young, he wanted to be a priest. But he came to Canada and fell in love with our mother.

We spent that summer sunning in the backyard. Helen would grab the tire swing and hurl it loose.

Joanne and I lay flat on the grass, fighting the urge to blink, watching it swoop towards us. The tire raced above us, rubber-smell fleeting and then blue sky.

We were there the day Irene came running out in her bare feet. She was wearing a white flowered dress, and her hair, wet from the shower, had soaked the back. My sisters and I stood up uncertainly when we saw her coming. She grabbed our wrists and dragged us into the house and upstairs to her bedroom. Through the window we saw our father turn into the alley, then drive straight onto the back lawn. He climbed out, forgetting to slam the car door behind him. We heard him running up the stairs. "Irene!" he yelled. "Irene!"

She looked at us. "Tom will be here soon."

"Irene!" Our father pounded the door with his fist. "Open this goddamned door!"

She shook her head at us. "He wasn't supposed to find out until later," she said. We stood beside the bed, next to her luggage, three plastic-shell suitcases, pale green, lined up all in a row. I went over to Irene and pulled at her arms, trying to get her attention. She looked past me, then stepped up to the door, unlocked it, and our father burst inside, his arms swinging. He was still in work clothes, suit pants and a white dress shirt. He was raging at Irene, saying, "I know, I knew it all along! You think I *didn't* know?" My father drove his fist into the closet door and the wood splintered. Then he turned around and grabbed the curtains and pulled them off the rod and the fabric balled up on the ground. We heard tires on gravel, turned to look through the window and saw Tom's car pulling up against the curb. Our father sank down, crying. "Do you know what I've put up with? Everything you do. All your crazy talk. Is this what I deserve?"

Irene folded her arms across her chest and stared at her feet. I wanted to go to my father but I could barely recognize him. His face was red and puffy, streaked with tears. We heard the front door open, Tom coming up the stairs. All of us listened to him and waited and then he was there. He held his back straight, looked right at Irene, and came into the room.

I thought my father would stand up, come at him, splinter his face the way he'd splintered the closet. He would tell Irene that enough was enough. But my father got to his feet, his face slick with sweat, and walked towards us. He crouched down to touch us but I backed away from him. My sister Helen said, "Dad, what's happening?"

He looked at her, his face old, suddenly. "You're going with them," he answered, his voice barely audible. "That's what your mother wants." He turned away from us and said to Irene, "Go wherever the hell you want." He never even looked at Tom.

Irene went to the window and watched him stagger down the back steps, walk across the lawn to the car. She screamed down at him to get out. She went over to the desk, picked up a stack of papers, old bills, letters, and flung them out the window. They showered the lawn. She kept screaming for him to get out, get out, even while he was reversing the car. Helen looked out the window and said, "He's left." Irene didn't hear. She pulled his clothes from the closet, shirts and pants tangled together, and threw them after him. Tom came and put his arms around her but she pushed him away. My sister Joanne ran out of the room, down the stairs, and out onto the back lawn, in the direction of our father's car. But Helen and I just stood there, watching in shocked silence. Helen turned to our mother and said, "What have you done?" Irene sat down on the bed, unmoving.

That night, we climbed into Tom's car. I was sitting up in the front seat, between Tom and Irene. Tom turned out of the driveway and I looked back at the house, all the lights left on.

Behind us, my sisters stared straight ahead, exhausted from the arguments and the yelling. They clutched their backpacks to their knees. "Mom?" Joanne said, when Tom pulled onto the highway and the city vanished behind a corridor of trees. "Mom?" Joanne said again.

"What is it?"

"Where are we going?"

Irene smiled, her face gentle. "Don't worry."

"I'm worried."

"Don't worry. We won't get there tonight."

"When?"

"Tomorrow night."

"How long are we going for?"

"Just a few days. I promise. Just a little while. I didn't think it would happen this way. But it's okay. I'm not angry."

Joanne leaned back rigidly in the seat. Beside her, Helen reached her arms out and held on to her.

Irene turned and watched them in the side mirror, her fingers tapping absently on the passenger-side window.

II

Irene was leaving our father because she was in love with Tom. In the car, she explained to us how she had married our father when she was nineteen. He was a good man, she said. He loved her very much and she had loved him. But now she was thirty, and he was thirty, and they had changed. She wanted to do what was best for us. "It's nobody's fault," she said, turning to look at me. "Everything will be okay." Tom drove straight ahead. On a winding road, he pulled over and Irene jammed her body out of the passenger door. She leaned over and threw up on the gravel.

My older sisters fidgeted in the back seat. Helen had a habit of biting her lips until they bled. She chewed her fingernails raw. She was forever picking at herself, pulling loose bits of skin from the corners of her mouth, her elbows and cuticles. Irene always said to let her be, she'd grow out of it one day. In the car, Helen nibbled angrily on her fingers. "Where are you *taking* us?" she said at one point, kicking the back of Irene's seat with her sneaker. Tom glanced at her in the mirror but no one answered. Joanne stared grimly out the window and I fell in and out of sleep, lying tipped over on top of Irene's legs. None of us spoke.

The clock on the dashboard read 1:00 by the time we got to Long Beach. Tom drove right up on the sand and parked the car. We couldn't see anything but the moon and the stars. Tom explained about the moon and gravity, how the tides were pulled in and out.

He turned to look at us. "Why the glum faces?" he asked. "You'll see. In the morning it will be beautiful." I had moved into the back seat by then, and my sisters and I were huddled together. Tom smiled. "Oh, I see," he said. "I can see what it's going to be like. You girls are a team, right? *Triple Trouble.*" He laughed out loud.

"Why don't you just shut up?" Helen said.

Irene stretched her arm out and touched him. "Not now. It's too late for jokes."

Tom lowered his chin. He got out of the car by himself, a gust of wind tearing through the open door, and began unloading the trunk. There was a big orange tent with metal poles that Tom assembled in the dark. Irene shone a flashlight out the car window, the beam tracing circles across the trees and the sky.

She spoke to the dashboard. "Don't tell anyone your names. Not for a little while yet, okay? Not until we sort things out."

Tom built a fire, tramping off into the night and returning with an armload of wood. We fell asleep in the car and Irene woke us, half dragging and half carrying us inside and tucking us into sleeping bags. We slept side by side all in a row: me between Irene and Tom, then Helen and Joanne. Tom had left the fire burning. Helen spoke up in the darkness. "That's a fire hazard. You better put it out."

"Enough," Irene said.

Tom turned over and faced the tent wall and all of us lay in silence.

We hated them so much it hurt. Helen kept a journal and she wrote: *Irene is not our real mother. Our real mother is living with our real father and we've been kidnapped by these hooligans. When the time is right, my sisters and I will run away.* We walked in single file along the beach, Joanne rushing ahead, Helen staying back to wait for me.

Together, we poked at sand dollars and starfish, combed the sand for unbroken shells. Helen said to me, "Do you understand what's happening?"

I nodded.

"We're moving. Do you know why?"

"Yes." I knew all too well.

"Don't worry," Helen told me, shaking her head. "We'll stick together. I'm going to take care of us." In front of us, Joanne ran in circles then collapsed into an angry ball. We sat beside her, watching the tide move in.

That first night on the beach, Tom shook his head at us, said, "What have you been up to all day? I was going to take you swimming." He showed us how to crouch down on our hands and knees and blow the fire so smoke rose thick from the wood. After dinner, Irene washed our hair under the cold-water tap, her fingers rubbing circles. She told us to go and dry by the fire and we stumbled away. Tom poked at the embers with a tree branch.

"How long will we stay here?" Helen asked.

Tom shrugged. "Who knows?"

"You shouldn't have brought us, then."

Irene stood behind us with her hands on her hips. "No," she said. "But it was either that or leave you altogether." Tom looked at her and Irene looked away, embarrassed.

Our mother slipped off her sandals and sat cross-legged on the ground beside us. She held out her arms for us but we just stood there, watching. She took hold of us and crowded us into her lap. We resisted at first but the smell of her seeped into our noses and her hair swung around and wrapped us in a dark cave. We held on to her too, our six hands grasping her wrists, her arms, anything we could reach. "It's only temporary," she said, kissing our hair. "Just to see. We'll wait a few days and then go home."

Tom said, "Wait a second, Irene —"

"They're my kids," she snapped. "They're mine, okay? I just want to wait and see."

Tom leaned towards us and touched her face with his thumbs. Irene shook her head and held us tightly. I wanted to run at him, stop thinking and push him down, fill his mouth with sand, push it up his nose until he stopped breathing. My whole body could be angry, mad as when Irene pushed the television over and the screen cracked and broke.

Tom unzipped the tent and crawled inside, Irene staring after him. The wind blew smoke from the fire all around us. "Wait for me here," she said, gently removing our hands. She crawled after Tom into the tent.

We watched smoke from the fire drift above our campsite, no sounds from either them or us. Every so often Joanne scratched at the dirt with her feet to say that we were still there. By the time Irene came out again, the trees were indistinguishable from the night. She poked at the fire with a branch, sending a gust of embers into the air.

We paced the beach. With the tide out, it seemed possible to walk forever. Other kids played with plastic shovels, dumped out bucket after bucket, ran ocean water through the moats of their castles. We wandered circles around them, taking stock of their clothes and their toys. I wanted to go home, even if it meant more of the same, Irene picking up the dishes one by one and throwing them out onto the back porch. Our father read the paper at the kitchen table. Sometimes when Irene screamed and screamed, he looked at her with complete incomprehension, not knowing why her face changed like that, why she scratched welts on her arms and then slid down against the wall like she was falling. Coming home from school, one of our friends cried when she saw the spoons and knives all over the floor, the bottles and the cracked dishes.

My sister Helen was the most pragmatic of us three. She said, "When we're sixteen, we can go home again."

Joanne stared morosely at her feet. That afternoon, she lay down in her shorts and T-shirt and we slowly buried her in sand.

During the days, my sisters and I avoided swimming in the ocean. Years ago, our father had taught us to swim. In a green lake, we floated on our backs, our bodies losing buoyancy. Our mother stood knee-deep keeping watch, pointing out to our father which one of us was going under, and he would pop us up as if we were weightless, keep us floating on the surface.

On our second night at the beach, we heard strange animal noises. Helen said it was a bear, pawing at our tent with his paws. Joanne tried to wake Irene but she just rolled over and sighed in her sleep. I dreamed Tom was sitting in the bathtub and I pushed the electric radio into the water. His body slapped against the bathtub. I watched in disbelieving silence until he died, his chest gray and shiny, sliding slowly underwater.

The next day, Irene forced us to go on a picnic. They took us to an outcrop of giant, black rocks where the tide came up in towering breakers. Tom said, "That's a whale," and pointed to where none of us could see. We sat at a nearby picnic table, chewing cold chicken and looking off into the distance.

Tom said, "Shall we go out a little farther?" Hand in hand, he and Irene walked up to the rocks, then climbed out on their hands and knees. At rest, they looked like seagulls, perched and waiting.

"Jerks," Helen said, her eyebrows tensed.

Behind us, Joanne walked silently through our picnic site. She was gathering things one by one — the glass bowl of potato salad, the two-liter bottle of orange pop, Irene's sunglasses.

"Are you making a run for it?" Helen asked.

Joanne ignored her. She climbed up onto the rocks above a shallow pool. Turning her back to us, she held the glass bowl out. Irene had just bought it, along with our groceries. It shimmered in the air. Joanne turned to look at us and her hands opened. The bowl tumbled down, cracking hard on a rock. She let go of the pop bottle. It fell upright, bouncing as it went. Then Irene's sunglasses.

I turned and saw Tom running towards the picnic site.

Joanne waved her empty hands. "Goodbye," she said. "Goodbye."

Tom was standing there, his mouth open. "What has gotten into you? For Christ's sake," he said, shaking his head. "For Christ's fucking sake." He picked up what was left and pushed past us to the gravel parking lot.

"For *Christ's fucking sake*," Joanne said.

Irene just stood and watched us, her expression calm. There were drops of water on her skin and the sun caught on them and made them glitter. She started to move closer but we stared her down. She stopped walking, brushed her foot in the dirt, and drew a line. Her voice was low. "You don't believe me now, but it's better like this. I know you think it couldn't be. You think nothing is worse than this. But believe me, there are worse things."

She put her arms around our shoulders and took us with her, back to the car.

Off the rocks and onto the gravel, I tried not to hear anything, not Tom or Irene or my sister's shoes on the rocks or the wind on the ocean or the rain starting to fall. We got into the car and Tom pulled roughly away from the parking lot.

After the car hit the highway, we were going fast and smooth. Tom said, "This is what I think. I think we should leave tomorrow. You don't think he'll follow us, right? You said so yourself, he doesn't give a damn. Four days is long enough. If he doesn't care, let's just go."

Our bodies fell together as if the car were tipping, one body slumped to the next. Irene's voice was barely audible. "Yes," she said, nodding. "Let's leave tomorrow."

Joanne was crying in the back seat. "How do you know?" she said. "How do you know he doesn't care?"

Helen put her hand on Joanne's head and stroked it back and forth. "Mom left a note. I saw it. He could come if he wanted to."

Tom looked sideways at Irene then back at the road.

"You have to tell us where we're going," Helen said. "It isn't fair to keep us in the dark."

"To stay with my sister," Tom said. "She has a cottage, right beside the ocean, just like here."

Irene's voice was barely audible. "Tom and I will take care of everything. When it's warm you can swim in the ocean. I'm going to get a job. In a store maybe. You'll meet all new kids."

"We already have friends," Helen said.

"New kids," Irene said, smiling stubbornly. "You'll make new friends."

Joanne shook her head. "We don't want new friends or a new school. You said we'd go back. You promised. You said we'd stay here a few days and then go home."

Tom cut in, "Look, it isn't easy for any of us."

"I don't know," Irene said.

"How come you can't keep your promises?"

"Don't talk to me that way."

"You *lied* to us. You said we'd go home."

"I didn't say that. I said maybe. Maybe isn't the same thing. And anyway it's too late to go back now."

"Why is it too late?"

"Because I've decided, okay?"

"You never asked us," Joanne said. "Maybe we would have stayed with him. Maybe we wouldn't have missed you. Do you understand? I miss him, maybe we wouldn't have missed you."

Irene didn't move. "I'm sorry," she said. "This wasn't the way it was supposed to happen."

She leaned towards Tom and then she half turned and her face was against his sleeve. We were waiting for her to lash out, to bang her fist against the window or throw something, smash the cassette tapes on the floor. But she stayed where she was and Tom patted her shoulder steadily. My sisters and I held still, as if we could change things by refusing to move.

The car hit eighty, ninety, one-twenty, and Tom looked sideways at Irene. He was nothing like our father. Tom's face was handsome and strong, and his hair, light blond, curled in tufts. Our father's face was dark and sad. Our father combed his hair with Brylcreem until it shone. He smelled of eucalyptus and cooking and warmth. But he and Tom looked at Irene with the same expression, mixed-up sadness and love and strange devotion.

Our last night on the beach, we listened to them breathing, the heaviness of it like their bodies were emptying out. We listened for animals, for a bear to come crashing through the trees. It could hear that breathing, we thought, and it would be drawn to us.

They said words aloud, mumbled like they were whispering secrets. She said, "Tom," and he started awake, put his arm around her.

Joanne complained that her stomach hurt. She pressed it with her fingers, wondered aloud if she had cancer, or if she were dying, slowly, in the middle of the woods and no one around. We heard other campers walking by, saw the finger-probe of their flashlights sliding across the tent, heard the trudge-trudge of their feet on gravel. I lay with my forehead pressed against Helen's neck. Every so often she would loop one arm across my shoulders, as if to reassure me.

Still Irene and Tom slept. Even when the ocean sounded so loud it seemed like it was coming right at us, all the land pushed under like a broken bowl, they slept, breathing heavily. We fell in and out of dreams, finally waking hours after they had risen. Tom slid the metal poles smoothly through the loops and the tent came down, the orange fabric floating like a parachute towards us.

III

On the fourth night, we arrived in North Bend. One by one, we climbed out of Tom's car. I remember

Irene standing in the motel parking lot looking over us. Tom had gone into the office alone to sign for the keys. The wind fanned Irene's hair out around her face and she looked at us, then down at her shoes, then back at us again. Standing under the motel lights, I thought none of this was real. Even then, I thought Irene would change her mind, she would take us home again and all of this would end.

They were standing in the motel room, their coats still on, when Irene broke down. Tom was walking from room to room, testing the light switches. "What will I do?" she said suddenly, raising her voice in desperation. "What have I done?"

Tom's voice was muffled in the background. Irene screamed that he had tricked her, he had made her come with him.

"Irene," he said. "Irene."

My sisters and I crept out the motel door, into the concrete parking lot. We stood beside Tom's car. Truthfully, I can't say that we were angry with her. Only that everything she was no longer surprised us. From where we stood we could see the ocean. If we looked down, we could see where it met the sky in a thin white line. The air smelled salty and cold. Finally, our mother came outside. "We'll go home," she was saying. "Tomorrow morning. We'll pack everything up and go home." She was looking past us, as if directing her words to the lights across the courtyard, to other people in other motel rooms. We didn't even bother answering. Helen reached over and held our mother around the waist. The top of her head was level with Irene's elbow. Joanne and I kicked at the gravel with our sneakers, sending the little rocks pinging off the cars. We heard the far-away whistle of a kettle going off and when we looked back, we saw Tom standing there, an outdoor lamp lighting his face, drawing fireflies to the air above him.

In the morning we woke up and found Tom and Irene sprawled together on the motel couch, their arms and legs tangled, Irene's hair spread out against Tom's hands.

This is my most vivid memory of my father: he was leaning over the veranda, his white shirt brilliant in the sun. Something about seeing him standing there, the neighborhood quiet in the background, made me want to confide in him. My father reached his hand down to rest on my shoulder. I held up the badminton birdie we had buried in mud. "Guess who gave this to me," I said.

My father raised his eyebrows.

"I got it from Tom."

"Tom who?" He took his handkerchief out and folded it once, then again.

"Tom from Sports and Leisure," I said. I explained that Tom came to visit all the time. And he brought us presents. Badminton rackets and bouncy balls. He and Irene sat up here in the afternoons, drinking and doing nothing. But I was sure that she liked him. The way she laughed all afternoon.

"Is that right?" my father said, after a moment. "And what do you think of Tom?"

I shrugged. "He's nice."

We stood quietly then, admiring the backyard. My father said he had always disliked the fence. It was made of cinder blocks stacked up one by one but he would much prefer a wooden gate. Then he turned and walked into the house. I stood looking at the yard. My sisters were playing on the tire swing, sitting spider, face-to-face, their arms and legs entwined. They swung back and forth and finally they looked up at me as if they knew what I had said, but they just kept swinging, the yellow rope extending out, my sisters hugging each other. I stood by myself, scared suddenly by what I had done.

When my father came home the next afternoon, and Irene forced us upstairs, I should have said then that I'd made a mistake, but I didn't. Irene started packing. She took the hot dogs from the freezer and threw them in with our T-shirts and sweaters. Tom had to do everything all over again. My sisters and I just sat and watched, nodding silently or shaking our heads, rejecting the extra sweater, accepting the crayons. Staring dumbly at Tom while he combed our hair and gave us grilled cheese sandwiches. I thought my father would return and everything would reverse itself. When Tom pushed the suitcase closed I started to cry. "I didn't mean it," I told Tom, hitting his chest with my fists. "I said I'm sorry. I didn't mean it." He picked me up and I kicked at him but it did no good. Irene kept bringing things out to the car, one box after another. Tom held on to me, though I was awkward, my arms and legs shooting out. I cried so hard his shirt was soaked. He whispered into my ear so that no one would hear, "I'm sorry. I'm sorry, too. I'm sorry," until I was finally quiet.

In the car, Tom took me with him into the front seat. When the car stopped at the intersections, he would look over at me without speaking. He would rest his hand on my knee, a moment of consolation, until the car began moving once more.

Eventually, it was Tom my sisters went to, instead of Irene. They told him about their boyfriends, the girls in school, the nights they crept out of the house and slept on the beach. They saw his sympathy, I think. When Irene had her breakdowns, they saw how he comforted her and didn't let go until she was well again.

My father had never been so patient with her, but even so, I yearned for him. I would try to get Irene to talk about him but she would shake her head, say, "Why do you ask me these things?" Once she asked me if I was trying, really trying to make her crazy, and another time, if I still had not forgiven her.

"This is the way things worked out," she said. "It does no good trying to imagine it differently."

From the time I was seven, I wrote to my father. His letters, though few and far between, were caring though restrained. After years of writing to him, I found it difficult to get past the first few sentences. *Dear Dad*, I'd write. *I hope you are keeping well.* I'd write about North Bend, or respond to the questions he asked about school. *Dear Dad*, I wrote once. *I am very sorry for everything that has happened*, but I never sent this letter. It was like writing a confession to someone from a dream. My father, himself, gave only the most general details of his life, and never asked for more from me. I can't blame him really. He probably still imagined me as a six-year-old child; he did not know me otherwise.

Not long ago, I said to Irene, "Did you ever know that I was the one who told? I was the one who gave everything away."

"If it wasn't you, it would have been one of the others." She shrugged. "It's over, in any case, and I'm not sorry."

I should have asked Irene why everyone else could pick up and go on, when that was the thing I found most difficult. Who left who, I often wondered. In the end, who walked away with the least resistance.

Over time, it was easy to love North Bend. That first year, we spent countless afternoons on the boulevard, watching the tourists. They moved in great, wide groups, clutching ice-cream cones and cameras. At the tourist office, they posed beside the World's Largest Frying Pan — the town's main attraction. The frying pan is sixty feet high and stands upright, wooden handle pointing to the sky. Tom told us it was given to the town in 1919, as a tribute to the women who stayed behind during the First World War.

Irene laughed and nodded her head. "It's big," she said, peering up along the carved wood handle. "A great big pan."

Come winter, the tourists disappeared and half the shops boarded up for the off-season. One afternoon, Tom ushered my sisters and me up to the frying pan and sat us down on the lip. The chill wind blew our hair all messy and Tom snapped a picture, the three of us hugging each other, laughing into the cold. Then we all started off along the waterfront, Tom closing his eyes and walking blindly across the sand. He let a gust of wind push him forward, his feet stumbling through the foam and water. We laughed, holding our arms out too, tossing about like dizzy birds, the wind tripping us up. Tom pretended to lose his balance, falling sideways on the ground, the freezing tide pouring over him. He sat up, laughing and spitting while we stood over his body, pretending to stomp him.

"No, no," Irene said. "You'll catch your death of cold."

We pretended to kick Tom in the stomach. "Enough!" he roared, leaping up, shaking foam and water from his head. My sisters and I scattered along the beach while he ran after us, Irene's voice barely audible in the background. "No! Stop it! Jesus Christ, be careful!"

That afternoon, he snapped close-ups of us, the lens of his camera inches from our faces, our hair tangling in front. Days later, he put a picture of Irene and the three of us up on the wall, my sisters and I transformed into bold sea creatures, the clouds and the sky brimming behind us. "What about you?" Helen asked, when we stood admiring the photograph. "Why didn't you put up one of you?"

"Me?" he said, laughing. "I'm just the photographer, nothing more."

Irene stared hard at the picture, her expression sad all of a sudden. She looked from Tom to us, as if from a great distance, then she turned and left the room. Tom did what my father had never done — he followed her, down the front steps, into the street. From inside, we could see the two of them standing together, heads touching, a moment of stillness, before they started back to the house.

One night, when Joanne was seventeen, she came home drunk and sick. She and Tom sat on the front steps all night. Her boyfriend, she wept, was sleeping with someone named Elsa, and had been for months. Joanne stomped up and down the stairs in frustration, then collapsed on the bottom step. "I don't even like him anyway," she sobbed, "so why does it hurt so much?"

Irene and I sat at the kitchen table, eavesdropping. There was no response from Tom.

Joanne told him she was sick of North Bend, sick of living by the water, the floods in winter. Listening to her, I thought of the groups of old men leaning their fishing lines out the back of their pickups, reeling fish in from the highway, how Joanne and I used to drive by and watch them. She told Tom she didn't know what to do next, thought alternately of running away, of drowning herself. There was no way she was going back to school.

"Why don't you run away, then?"

She started crying again. "Why do you want me to leave?"

Tom's voice was tired. "It's not a lack of love. I don't want you drowning. That's all." He gave her five hundred dollars right there. Irene didn't interfere. She sat at the kitchen table, letting Tom do what he thought was right. In the morning Joanne packed her things and left, caught a bus straight out of Oregon and headed north. My sister Helen moved out not long after. She'd met a bio-technologist from Vancouver and married him. We threw a big party for her at the house, then they drove away to Canada.

These days, our town is visited by many tourists. They come from far and wide. On a Saturday during the busy season, the cars hail from every state, from Alaska to New Jersey, and from all across Canada.

I am in charge of the walking tours, the 9:30, 12:15, and 3:00 groups. We start at the town hall and head east along the boulevard, past Flotsam & Jetsam, the Whale's Tail, and Circus World, with its natural and unnatural artifacts — fish dishes, glass buoys, bone fossils. Circus World boasts the skeleton of a half-goat, half-human boy, mounted in a glass case. For one dollar, you can buy a snapshot of him and send it, postage paid, anywhere in the country. The tour ends at the big frying pan.

It's the *why* of it that nobody understands. I tell my father's version of the story, the frying pan as war memorial, erected as a tribute to the women who stayed behind. Then I tell my mother's version, the frying pan for the sake of the frying pan, one monumental gesture. North Bend's Eiffel Tower, the wooden handle visible for miles.

The Japanese tourists giggle, cupping their hands to their mouths. But the big East Coast men with Hawaiian shirts and baseball caps tell me, "You can never have a thing too big. We've got the skyscrapers, you know. Sky*scrapers*. Unbelievable." They tilt their heads back then, and focus on the air above.

Tom and Irene own a sporting-goods store in North Bend, selling things like scuba gear, flippers, and surfboards. In the mornings, Tom takes a walk inland, just for the pleasure of turning around again and walking downhill to the ocean. Irene stands on the front steps looking out for him. She has a longing for him. I could be standing right beside her and she wouldn't even know me.

I am thirty years old and I don't know if I will ever leave this town. I should, of course, just to see the world. But I would want to come back here. Some changes happen so slowly, you can't know until it's done — my parents aging, the beach washing back from the water. Maybe when I am sixty, the town itself will have receded. All of us who stay here will creep backwards too, watching and watching for change, then being surprised when it strikes us, out of the blue. No reason but the fact that it is all different. In our house uphill from the ocean, Irene and Tom and I sit in the kitchen reading books and magazines. From morning until night we can hear the water and the wind and the two mixing together. At night, I can hear their voices through the walls, and the past finally seems right in its place. Not everything, not large, but still present.

Alchemy

In my memory, I followed Paula to the end of the aisle, past the hair products, shampoos, the colored lights, through an empty mall, a parking lot, Granville Street at night with kids and adults panhandling, to a bus all lit up, down a quiet street to her house, where she closed the door behind her, smiling. I stood on the lawn outside. From there I could see everything: the back shed, the porch with the rabbit hutch, her open window with the blue curtains billowing out. Before disappearing she had said, "The rabbits are gone," and I understood that as a sign. *Move on,* she was telling me. *I'm on my own now.* So I left her.

I remembered that last night. I had wanted a sign from Paula. Not everyone believes in signs. But the more you need them, the more you see and the more you believe. I found a white hair today and pulled it out. I call that a sign. After all, sixteen is young.

In school we've been learning about time. How human beings have hardly put a dent in it. If the history of the earth were mapped against a single year, we would only show up on December 31, at 4:11 in the afternoon. I would have told Paula that, and we would have mulled it over late at night. We would have laughed and said that, in the history of the earth, she and I, her father and mother and Jonah, were nothing. They would fall away from us without a bruise or a scratch. We could blow them off our bodies. We could say, with confidence, that in the grand scheme of things, in the long run, they meant as little as dust. "Less," Paula would say. And I would say, "Less."

Paula's mom worked downtown at the Hotel Vancouver. She was a housekeeper and smelled of fresh sheets and mild sweat. She always came home first, hung her coat neatly in the closet, unbuttoned the first three buttons of her blouse, and started cooking. Paula's father was a gruff yet caring man. He fixed cars for a living, came home with grease under his fingernails and the smell of oil on his skin.

I preferred Paula's home to mine and so I stayed over at her house most nights. At dinner, Paula's dad once said to me, "Do you know how much it costs to keep an extra body, Miriam? Tell your parents to pay up."

Her mom made a noise like, "Ssss, shush." Paula stared at her plate, motionless. Her dad shook his head, apparently hurt, and picked up his knife and fork. "Eh, Jesus. I'm kidding, okay? Can't I do that in my own home? Any friend of Paula's is welcome here." The four of us ate quietly. Paula's mom brought out drinks, cola for me and Paula, Molson's for her dad, water for herself. She brought out dessert, a Boston cream pie, leftover from the hotel kitchen that day.

Afterwards, in the bathroom, I stood back while Paula threw up dinner. Her hair, bleached blond, stuck to her face. She rinsed her mouth and said, "I only throw up dinners. You only have an eating disorder if you throw up everything." Paula told me that there were four kinds of bodies: the X, the A, the Y, and the O. "You're an X," she said, "small waist and evenly proportioned chest and butt." She turned sideways. "What do you think I am?"

"An X."

"Wrong," she smirked. "Nice try. I'm more of an A. Heavy on the bottom." She picked up my wrist and measured it with her fingers. Her thumb and index finger touched. "You're lucky. Everyone wants to be an X."

We stayed up late, talking about Jonah and how the halls were empty because the senior boys had gone away to play basketball and about how our math teacher had hair growing on his back. If you stood behind him, you could see it push past his collar, a hairy finger. Paula and I pressed our faces into the pillows and laughed. A breeze came and blew her curtains back into the room, light from a passing car travelling down the wall, across our beds, and gone. She said, "Move in here. Why don't you just move into the spare bedroom? If you hate your family so much, you might as well, don't you think?"

"I don't hate them."

"Well, whatever. You hardly go home anyway."

"I'll ask," I said, though I knew I wouldn't. In my home, we barely spoke. My parents had long since given up on their marriage. They were busy working, making ends meet, and hardly noticed whether I was home or not.

"We could be sisters then." Paula lay back on her pillow. "We'll share everything."

Paula wanted to be a veterinarian. That meant that, after dark, we'd slip out of her house and into the backyard, where her mom kept hutch rabbits. Once a week, at supper time, her mom pulled one or two from the cage, broke their necks, skinned their bodies, and drained the blood in the kitchen sink. She made rabbit stew, simmering the meat until it was tender, and you could smell the potatoes and carrots and meat all through the house and down the street.

The first time we snuck outside, Paula unlatched the door and poked her face up to the cage. "Be free," she whispered. "Be free or be stew." The rabbits came and stood in the long grass, their noses twitching. We lay down, and they crawled timidly on top of us, onto our heads. "They like our hair," Paula told me. "They feel safe there." She tried to coax them across the backyard, crouching on her hands and knees, leading the way to the fence. But they were nervous and would only take a few loping steps before something scared them, a bird overhead, a motorcycle on Knight Street. They scampered back to their hutch.

"What can we do?" Paula asked. "They're not wild, after all."

We stayed out on the back lawn listening to the traffic. At one point, a light came on in the kitchen and we froze. Paula's dad stood at the window, a glass of water in his hand. He took forever to drink it, staring straight at us through the glass, but we trusted the dark and willed ourselves invisible. When the light in the kitchen went off, we breathed easy again, felt the chill in the wind, came back to life.

The nights I slept over, I would wake up with my face in Paula's hair. It leaped away from her, full of static. The smell would wake me up, apples and dish soap and sweat. I wondered what it would be like to wake up beside someone night after night, hair in your face, legs crossing heavily under the blankets. If the smell and feel would tire you out, like it had my mom and dad. They slept in separate rooms, Mom on the couch and Dad in the bedroom. Sometimes they sat in the same room though neither of them would acknowledge the other. They had perfected it, made it an art to see something but believe it wasn't there.

Once, when Paula and I were lying in bed, she asked me, "Are you a virgin still?"

"Of course," I said, thinking of Jonah. I stared at her fingers on the top of the blanket, spread out and still. "Aren't you?"

She lifted her hands, holding them over our heads like planets, constellations, something we'd never seen up close. "I'm not sure," she said.

We lay together quietly under the blankets. For a long time lying there, I wondered if I should say something more, but then the moment passed. I could hear her breathing grow heavier. Before she fell asleep, she turned over and held on to me. Her grip was so plaintive that I felt sorry for her and held on, too. I had the sense that some things were impossible for her to say.

In school, we'd been learning about species. We had to imagine billions of years, different species rising like bubbles to the surface, all this time passing. But I could not imagine ten years, fifteen, twenty. My sixteen years felt like eternity but I knew I wouldn't be like this forever. In all my life, the total sum of it, I was a species rising and falling. One day I would wake up and all of it would be gone.

At first, when Paula and I talked about Jonah, we were conspirators. Together, we laid out a course of action. She made sure I stood behind him at the line-up in the cafeteria, that I sat in front of him in French class, that we happened by his locker three times a day, every day. She planned out the life we might have and whispered it to me in the hallway, one hand excitedly grasping my elbow. He would take me into his confidence, slowly. He would unburden secrets he never shared with anyone. A long time in the future, he might kiss me.

One day Jonah appeared in front of my locker and said, "Let me drive you home, Miriam." Outside my parents' apartment, below their window, he put his car into neutral and reached over, running his hand from my chin to my stomach. I leaned into him. He kissed me, and I felt like I was being pushed to the bottom of a swimming pool, everything distorted, unfocused yet clear as glass. I felt myself moving through years and years, coming up different all of a sudden.

Once, in P.E. class, I watched Jonah running laps. He was falling behind, the other boys were far ahead of him, but he kept on, one hand grasping his chest then blurring down. He ran past me, breathing hard, but he blew me a kiss from the center of the palm of his hand. When I sat in front of him in French class, sometimes he whispered small requests, an eraser, an extra pen, and I passed them back without looking. But how I loved to look at him. He had dark hair and his eyes were round and dark and lovely. He had a soft body, not pounded immovable by sports, just regular and wide and comfortable.

Paula smirked when I told her this. She said, "That isn't any reason to love someone."

"It is for me."

She bent her head down. Now that Jonah had entered my life, she no longer approved of him. "Don't say I didn't warn you. You don't know what you're getting into."

"Then tell me."

She looked at me, her face blank, then turned and left. I didn't follow.

Later on, when Jonah and I slept together in his bedroom, I imagined looking down on us from the ceiling, I pictured how dark and naked our bodies must be, how small the two of us were. Right then I wanted to tell Paula that there are some things you have to go through on your own. Some relationships withstand life, some are there for a moment, a stepping stone, and then you push away from them.

But I never did because Paula said, "Don't talk to me about Jonah. I don't want to know."

"I won't tell you anything then."

"I thought you were going to move in here. I thought you were unhappy at home and you wanted to live with me." She lay down on her bed, yellow hair spreading in a circle. We had learned about Joan of Arc, and I imagined holding a match to Paula's hair; it was so dry it would catch in an instant, sprout into a ball of flame. "Don't lie to me any more," she said. "Just say whether you will or not."

"I have my own family, Paula."

Some part of her seemed to give way. "But I need you here."

"Why?" I said, exasperated.

She turned away. "Go home then. I don't want to see you."

I wanted to tell Paula what was happening, how one thing leads to another. How a boy like Jonah feels like a necessary thing. He has a way about him, like a curved handle, so easy to hold, so easy to see. He can smile and something flares up in you, catches on your heart, opens you up to things you wanted but never asked for. He can change the way your mind forms words, shapes sentences, imagines their capacity. He has a heart you think you can drink from. I've heard that it's common, there are lots of boys, and girls too, who are like this. Their faces have promise in them, but how can you be promised something you will never stop wanting?

Once, after Jonah and I had sex, he said, "You really like it, don't you? It scares me how much you like it." He smiled at me knowingly, and I nodded. I never knew what to say.

I slept at Paula's house less and less. At school, she would corner me in the bathroom and ask me to come over. I never gave firm answers. I was waiting for Jonah to come by, sweep me into his car, forgive me. It seemed like I was always doing something wrong — I held him too tightly, told him I loved him. It never came out right. When I said it, the words sounded more like a plea.

"I'll see," I told Paula.

She nodded her head. Her hair was a different shade. Clairol "Stardust," she told me. She was losing weight, too, and it made her face thin and freakish.

I did go over, and that night we lay outside on the back porch, the stars muted by the city lights. She said, "I've been thinking about running away." She had her eyes closed as if she were imagining it right then, some new place farther inland, a new city identical to this one, but different in all the right ways.

Sometime after midnight, she stood up and walked slowly down the back steps. When she returned, she was carrying the cage of hutch rabbits. We lay on the deck watching them, then Paula undid the latch. Reaching in, she lifted the rabbits out one by one until all five sat shivering on the deck. "Go," she said, waving towards the stairs. "This might be your last chance." They stayed where they were, frozen by the traffic sounds and the half moon. Paula leaned down and blew on each of them gently. They crept forward. "Go on." They froze.

She gathered the nearest one in her arms. Then she stood and walked across the veranda, the rabbit bundled against her chest. At the railing she stopped, stretched her arms out, and held it straight in front of her. There was laundry on the line, shirts pinned up like paper cut-outs. A light came on in her parents' bedroom. Paula opened her arms. I saw the rabbit falling slowly.

The traffic on Knight Street kept going by and going by. She ran down the back stairs. I heard her say, "Oh no," in a flat voice. I didn't look. I gathered the other four and put them back in the hutch. Paula laid a piece of newspaper on the concrete walkway, overtop of the one she had dropped. She looked up at me and said, "My fingers slipped."

I said, "It's okay. There are lots of others."

That night, in the middle of sleep, I heard voices, a man and a woman. They were whispering, and he was impatient with her. I thought I felt Paula get up and leave me but when I woke up in the night I was confused because it was only the two of us in her bedroom. Paula had one arm across my waist; she had her face buried against my arm.

Jonah came over to my house twice a week and I helped him with his science homework. We memorized the periods of the geologic time scale, traded them back and forth as if they were codes. "Triassic, Jurassic, Cretaceous, Tertiary, Quaternary," he giggled. I laughed with him.

We sat with our legs dangling out the window, and I said again, "I love you." He looked at me, his face confused. "How do you know?" he asked.

"I just do."

He said, "You're crazy."

When he lay on top of me I looked up at him and willed myself to feel joyous, exuberant, but it was like something on the other side of the world. He caught my eye for a moment and I saw an expression pass across his face. Afterwards, I tried to name what I saw. Pity, perhaps, more pity than love.

When Jonah left, I walked to Paula's house. At Knight Street, I stood on the curb. My mom said this was the most dangerous street in the city, all the semis, four-by-fours, speed demons. I thought of walking into the street. But I wasn't brave enough to do a thing like that. Standing on the sidewalk, the traffic whipping my hair from my face, I felt the sensation of flight.

Paula's house was just around the corner. I walked across her front lawn, then rapped on the window. When she opened the door and saw me, she didn't look at all surprised. She poured two glasses of brandy and we watched *Mask,* a movie with Cher and a boy who had the elephant-man disease. The sun went down through the window behind the television set; it filled the glass and steeped the room in sunlight. In the movie, Cher fights for her son because she loves him so deeply it cuts her open. Paula filled our glasses again and again. The bottle shone like a coin in the room.

Paula turned to face me. She said, "I've got the other bedroom all set up."

I could feel the brandy slipping down my throat, holding in my chest, and pumping warmth like a spare heart. "I told you, Paula. I have my own home."

She looked taken aback, then she nodded. "We're best friends. Even best friends don't tell each other everything."

Paula took another drink and looked at me thoughtfully. Then she pointed through the window at the back shed. "See that? I used to fix cars in there with my dad. I'd lie on my back on one of those trolleys, and he'd roll me under. It's lonely under there, and dark. And then one day I just stopped going. My mom said to me, 'What's the matter with you? Don't be so lazy. Your father needs your help.' I told her that I didn't want to go to the shed, I didn't want to be with him. I was too old to go there."

I looked down at the carpet, shaking my head. The alcohol faded through me in a slow wash. "Paula," I said. "Stop talking."

"My mom told me, 'This is how families fall apart.' I didn't want to believe her, but I did. So I kept going back. I can't stop it. I think maybe I'm the one who's sick. Sometimes I go into the shed and roll myself underneath the car and I pretend I've been hit and I'm lying in the road, almost dead. Just in case, just so I know beforehand what it might feel like."

I knew what was coming next and I didn't want to hear it. I shook my head to block her out.

"Listen to me. It doesn't matter who you fuck or how you do it. It's all the same, it always hurts. Why won't you just stay here? If you were here, this wouldn't happen."

I hit her across the mouth to stop her. A loose

hit, palm flat, the smack high-pitched. Her mouth fell open.

She shook her head, hysterical. "I'm not lying."

"You shouldn't let him." I couldn't look at her when I said it. "Why do you let him do it?" Then I stood and walked stiffly across the living room, down the hallway, to the front door. Paula's mother came awkwardly to the top of the stairs, her weight pulling her side to side. "What's wrong?" she asked. "Who's crying?"

I shook my head and pulled on my shoes. Paula's voice rose higher and higher. Her mom said, "Paula?" and ran down the stairs, one hand pressed to the opening in her nightgown. When I opened the front door to leave I could hear Paula sobbing, "Leave me alone. Please, just leave me alone."

I started walking, past Kingsway and onto Slocan where the traffic lights disappeared and the street was soft in darkness. I slowed down, paid attention to each car sliding by, the lights settling on me for half a second.

A man in a car drove up beside me. He pushed his head out the window, whistling. "Beautiful," he said. I turned and stared at him. He smiled, motioning me towards him.

I went towards his car, all the feeling in me lost. I opened the passenger door and thought, this is what it all comes to. I'd seen pictures of girls like me, here one moment then gone the next. When I climbed into the car, I thought of Paula sitting on the floor in her living room, face in her hands, her mom's arms wrapped around her. Paula's expression when I turned away from her. We eased away from the curb and he said, "Where are you going?"

I told him I was going home.

"Do you want to go there?"

I nodded.

He smiled knowingly. "Are you sure?"

"Yes."

He turned the radio on and let one hand drift over to rest on my thigh. I thought, everything has led to this. This is what it comes to.

But he drove me home. He let his car idle behind my parents' apartment building. When I put my hand on the door handle, he said, "Let me kiss you."

I looked him full in the face and saw he was older, so much older than me. He leaned towards me, and I remembered what Paula said. It doesn't matter who or how. I turned my face to him, the street empty and the car warm. He kissed me, and I felt his moustache on my skin, a passing touch. Then I got out of the car and walked home.

The next morning, Paula ran away. She left her house as usual, carrying only her school bag, and didn't come home. I learned later, from Paula's mother, that she had left a note in the kitchen, telling her mother that she would take care of herself and not to worry.

In the spring, once or twice, I walked by Paula's house. From the outside it looked the same, the windows in her bedroom open and the blue curtains moving gently in the breeze. We had picked the material for the curtains at Fanny's Fabrics and Paula's mom had sewn them exactly as Paula had wanted. I stood on the sidewalk out front hoping that wherever Paula was, they would never find her and make her go home again.

Once, Jonah lay his hand against my neck, and I was startled. He said, "Sometimes I look at you and you are very beautiful." I wondered if he meant to be terrible or if there were some truth in this, a tiny piece, but too little to buy happiness, security, love. I held on to him and felt my mind, my heart, and my body separating. Wherever Paula was, I wondered if she had come across the formula that would keep these parts intact, if the act of leaving had taught her some truth I still could not grasp. After Jonah left, I sorted through the mail but nothing came.

In the weeks after Paula ran away, a counselor and a youth officer at our school called us to their office one by one. They pulled me out of Geography class, and my stomach filled up with dread. In their tiny room, I sat as still as possible, staring at the floor. The police officer was at the back. Paula's mom was there too, foreign-looking in her work clothes, blouse and pleated blue skirt, nylons and black moccasins. She touched me gently, one hand against my back, then she went and sat in the corner.

The counselor smiled at me. She said, "We want to help Paula just as much as you do, Miriam."

"I haven't heard from her."

"Do you know where she might have gone?"

"No."

"Do you have any idea why she left?"

I shook my head.

The counselor poured coffee into a styrofoam cup, then stood and circled the room, offering the pot to the officer and then Paula's mom. They both covered their cups with their hands and shook their heads and everyone sat in silence. Paula's mom whispered, "Surely you know something. Can't you guess where she is?"

The school counselor caught my eye. "Her parents are very worried. We're all very worried about her safety."

I said, "I don't know."

Paula's mom said, "But she told you everything."

This startled me. I looked down at my hands, thinking of Paula, the two of us stretched out on her living-room floor, the brandy flooding us with warmth. How when I left her house that night, that warmth evaporated. I thought we had both known the truth, but Paula was the only one brave enough to say it then, and not me. "A few months ago," I said, "I slept over at Paula's house. I woke up in the night and her father was standing beside our bed. He was touching her hair. He had his hand over her face. She turned away from him and held me and later on I woke up and she was crying, but I pretended I was asleep."

I folded my hands in my lap and looked up. "What do you think it meant?" No one answered me. I said, "I know that in her own house, Paula was always afraid to sleep alone."

I looked up at the woman because I was afraid she wouldn't believe me. I held her gaze and felt a humming in my chest like a burst note.

When I left the office Paula's mom followed me out into the hallway. Her face was coming apart and she said, "What are you trying to do?" I stared at her hair, curly brown and wisping to gray. She said, "How can you do this? How dare you lie like that?" and I felt blank, an opening inside where the humming was, dead air.

I turned and walked down the hallway, leaving her standing there alone. I didn't know what difference I made — if the truth would be of any use to Paula now, or if it was too late. But I believed her. I had believed her from the start and this was the only thing I knew how to do.

I remembered Paula buying hair color in the drugstore. She couldn't decide between one and the other,

Clairol "Brash" or Nice & Easy "Natural Light." I was impatient and said, "Let's go, Paula. They're all the same." She balanced them, one in each hand, as if she could tell by the weight. She glared at me. I thought, if you could change your life with a shade of color, if it had ever been that easy, we would not be standing here in the first place.

I waited for Paula to write me. I kept in my head a list of things I would tell her. How her house was the same as ever but they left her bedroom window open, as if hoping one morning she would climb back in again. That grade eleven was the same as grade ten. That things got a lot worse before they got any better. We had learned the history of gold. How people had rushed up the coast, panning for it, because they believed that the nuggets might be as abundant as the fish. And long ago, people tried to make something out of nothing, filling beakers with coins and the seven metals made from seven planets, how they hung their hopes on this, like a coat rack.

Then, I only hoped. Because Paula did not write and I did not know where she was, I tried to dream it. I imagined a place of great abundance. Fish in the seas and terrible beauty.

Dispatch

The way you imagine it, the car is speeding on the highway. Over Confederation Bridge, streetlamps flashing by. It's early spring and the water below, still partially frozen, shines like a clouded mirror. You saw this bridge on a postage stamp once. It is thirteen kilometers, made of concrete, and it is not straight. It curves right and left so that no one will fall asleep at the wheel. In the morning sunshine, the concrete is blindingly white.

"Here we go," Heather, the driver, says. She has a calm, collected voice.

Charlotte — you saw a picture of her once, dark-brown hair tied in a low ponytail — has her feet propped up against the dashboard. Her toenails are lacquered a deep sea blue. In the back seat, Jean leans forward, nodding appreciatively at the coastal landscape. The earth is red, the way they imagined it would be. It is rolling and the colors segue together, red and coffee brown and deep green. A flower garden on a hill shapes the words *Welcome to New Brunswick*.

Beside the road there are cows standing in a circle, heads together, like football players in a huddle. Charlotte points through the windshield at them. "Strange sight," she says. Her words get lost under the radio and the engine accelerating, but the other two nod and laugh. They wave to the cows. The car is shooting down the highway, trailing over the yellow line and back again, down to a curve in the stretch of road where they slip out of sight.

This country is a mystery to you. The farthest east you have been is Banff, Alberta. To imagine these three women then, Charlotte and Heather and Jean, you have to make everything up as you go. Take Atlantic Canada, for instance. You remember postcards of white clapboard churches, high steeples glinting in the sun. You've never met Charlotte, but you picture yourself with the three of them, driving by, snapping pictures. Along winding dirt roads, they chance upon coastal towns, lobster boats bobbing on the water. Or else abandoned canneries, paint bleached and peeling, the wood still smelling like the sea.

Instead of working, you daydream or sit cross-legged on the couch roaming the television channels. For you, news is a staple food. There's a story about a freighter that sprang a leak crossing the Atlantic Ocean. Thousands of boxes fell into the water. Months later, the cargo — a load of bathtub toys — washes up on the shoreline. Children and adults comb the beach. "I am six and three-quarters years old," one boy tells the cameras proudly. "I have collected fifty-three rubber ducks." He smiles, his pockets and hands overflowing with yellow.

You're writing a book about glass, the millions of glass fishing floats that are travelling across the Pacific Ocean. They come in all shapes, rolling pins, Easter eggs, perfect spheres. And the colors, cranberry, emerald, cobalt blue. In North America, these glass floats wash up in the hundreds. Decades ago, boys and girls ran to gather them in, the buoys shimmering at their feet. They sold them for pocket money. Now, the floats are harder to come by. In the wake of storms, collectors pace the beach. Every so often, a rare one appears. Recently, on Christmas morning, a man and his granddaughter came across a solid black orb. Shine it as he did, the glass float remained dark as a bowling ball. The float has no special markings and, to date, its origins are unknown.

For hours, you stare at the computer screen thinking about the load of bathtub toys. You have far too much time on your hands. Sometimes a thought settles in your mind like a stray hair and refuses to leave. Like now, you remember your husband coming in after a jog in the rain. He went straight into the bathroom. When you heard the sound of water drumming against the bathtub, you snuck inside, steam and hot air hitting your lungs. For a full minute, you watched your husband shower, his back to you. The skin on your face broke into a sweat. You watched his body, the runner's muscles, the tendons. You reached your hand out and placed it flat against his spine, where the vertebrae curved into sacrum. He didn't even startle.

You think now that he always knew you were there. You think of the million ways he could have read this gesture. But what did you mean, putting your hand out? Perhaps you only wanted to surprise him. Perhaps you only wanted to see if through the steam and heat he was truly there, or just a figment of your imagination.

Sometimes when they're driving, no one wants to stop. Like they're married to the highway, the exit signs flashing past. They're thousands of exits away from Vancouver.

It's food that lures them off the road. A Tim Horton's at the side of the highway, beckoning. You watch them giggle into a booth, styrofoam cups of coffee balanced in their trembling, stir-crazy fingers. The first half-dozen doughnuts go just like that. Heather lines up for more. "Get the fritters," Jean says, laughing, her voice shrill in the doughnut shop. "I just *love* those fritters." Heather buys a dozen. They're sugar-crazed by the end of it, strung out on the sidewalk in front, their legs stretched in front of them.

At night, the three of them pile into a double bed. "I've forgotten what the rest of my life is like," Heather says. They've each written up a handful of postcards, but have yet to send them off.

Charlotte lies back on her pillow. Her hair has come loose from its elastic band and it floats down beside her. "Don't you ever wonder what it would be like *not* to go back?"

"If I had a million dollars," Heather says.

"Don't you ever think, though, overland, we could drive to Chile. If we just started going in a different direction. Instead of going west, we could be in Chile."

The next morning they continue west and no one complains. Outside Thunder Bay, they pull over at the statue of Terry Fox. Charlotte sits down on the stone steps and cries. She can't stop. "It's the fatigue," she tells them, struggling to catch her breath. "God, I'm tired of sleeping in motel rooms every night.

Let's pull out the tents and camp. To hell with indoor plumbing. Can't we do that?" The tears are streaming down her face, mascara thick on her cheeks.

Later on, in the dark of their tent, she tells them how she remembers the day he died. When she describes it — how she stood at her elementary school in a jogging suit, listening to the announcement on the radio, watching the flag lowered to half-mast — she feels her life coming back to her. Bits and pieces she thought were long forgotten. Before that moment, she was too young to fully understand that death could happen. But then the young man on the television, the one with the curly hair and the grimace, he died and it broke her heart.

Your husband has the body and soul of a long-distance runner. He is a long-haul kind of man. Even asleep, he has that tenacity. At a moment's notice, he'll be up again, stretched and ready. Unlike you. When you lie down, you doubt your ability to up yourself again. You are the Sloppy Joe of women. You watch TV lying on the couch, you read in bed, curled up on one side. Sometimes, when the lights are out, you drag your computer into bed with you. While your husband snores, you write about the woman who owned four thousand glass floats. An arsonist torched the building she lived in. The apartment collapsed but, miraculously, no one was killed. The morning after, passers-by came and picked the surviving balls from the rubble — black and ashy and melted down.

At night, in the glow of the screen, you type to the up, down of your husband's breathing. It's difficult to look at him in these moments. His face is so open, so slack-jawed, vulnerable and alone. Both of you have always been solitary people. Like big cedars, your husband says, bulky and thick, growing wider year by year. You are charmed by your husband's metaphors, the quiet simplicity of them.

Your husband has never been unfaithful to you. But only a few months ago, you found the letter he had written to Charlotte. They had grown up together and, in the letter, he confessed that he loved her. Your husband left the letter, and her reply, face up on the kitchen table. You imagine the instant he realized, standing on the warehouse floor, broom in one hand. He tried to call you, but you just stood there, letting the telephone ring and ring. When you read his confession on that piece of looseleaf, your husband's perfect script stunned you. You thought of his face, his brown eyes and the receding slope of his hairline, the way he sat at the kitchen table reading the paper, frowning, his lips moving silently to read the words.

The woman, Charlotte, had written back. She had told him to pull himself together. She'd returned his letter, telling him that their friendship would never recover. And then he left both letters on the kitchen table. Not maliciously. You refuse to believe he did it maliciously. Your husband is not that kind of man. He is the kind of person who honors privacy, who can carry a secret until the end. Shell-shocked and hurt, he must have forgotten everything.

You've imagined it perfectly. Before he left for work, he took both letters and laid them on the kitchen table. He read them over and over. He'd offered to leave his marriage for her, but she had turned him down flat. *Pull yourself together.* He made a pot of coffee and poured himself a cup. He put on his shoes, then his jacket. The envelope was on the counter. He folded it up and tucked it in his pocket. Hours later, while his mind wandered back and forth, he pulled it out, only to discover the envelope was empty. The letters were still face up on the kitchen table, where his wife, sleep-creased and hungry, had found them. He called, but the phone just rang and rang.

That night, you went out and didn't come home. You climbed on a bus and crossed the city, crying intermittently into the sleeve of your coat. At a twenty-four-hour diner, you ordered a hamburger and fries and sat there until dawn, when the early risers started showing up for breakfast. You read the paper from the night before, and then the paper from that day, cover to cover, and then you walked home, through the tree-lined streets and the slow muscle of traffic heading downtown. At home, your husband was already gone. You turned on the TV, then you lay down in bed and slept for hours.

You've pictured it from beginning to end, upside and down, in every direction. You've pictured it until it's made you sick and dizzy. Your husband has never been unfaithful to you, but something in your life is loose now. A pin is undone. When he came home and lay down beside you, you told him, "We'll work things out," and he, ashen-faced, nodded.

His skin was pale in the white sheets and you hovered above him, kissing his skin, trying not to miss anything. You have never been unfaithful. That's what you were thinking every time you kissed him. Look at me, you thought. I have never been unfaithful, and here I am, kissing you. You looked straight at him. Your husband's heart was broken and it wasn't you who did it. That's what you thought, when he pushed his face against your chest, his body taut and grieving.

There's a memory in your mind that you can't get rid of. The two of you in bed, lying next to one another like fish on the shore, watching images of Angola. Out on Oak Street there's the white noise of traffic, endlessly coming. Catastrophe. Your husband said that line again, "Too many cameras and not enough food," and the two of you watched a woman weep.

She wiped her eyes in her dirty handkerchief. And you, on the other side of the world, on another planet, watched soundlessly.

Instead of writing your book, you are watching the midday news. Like some kind of teenage kid, you're lying on the couch, the remote cradled on your stomach, hand in the popcorn. The world is going to hell in a handbasket. You think this but never say it aloud because it's terrible to be so cynical. But look at the world. While your city works its nine-to-five, bombs detonate, planes crash, accidents happen. You sound like your mother. While your marriage stutters on, revolutions rise and fall, blooming on the midday news like some kind of summer flower. There's dinner to be made. Lately you have discovered your weak heart. Instead of sitting at the kitchen table writing your book, you're watching flood waters in Central America, you're watching Dili, people in trucks with rifles strung on their arms. You've never even heard a shot fired. You know you think about your marriage far too much. You know that, given the chance, you will sit all day on your couch like this, watch what happens in another country. There is a woman clinging to a rooftop. A flood in Mozambique. A lack of supplies, everything coming too late. By morning, the water may rise over the spot where she sits. You want to get on a plane. You who have always wanted to please people, you want to sandbag and work. You know what you think of this woman on the rooftop — she did nothing to deserve this. But what would she think of you? She would look at you with disbelieving eyes. She would look at you with only the faintest expression of pity.

Through small-town Ontario, the three women snap photos of water towers. While you watch from the background, Charlotte climbs through the passenger window, her body swaying recklessly out. When she ducks back in, her hair is wild, blown frizzy around her head. She smiles a lopsided grin.

Past hockey arenas and high-steepled churches, blue sky over dry fields, they're singing along to the radio. Looking forward to night, when they will pitch their tent under cover of stars, break out the beer bottles which clank in the trunk. They can see themselves dancing carelessly in the hot evening. Charlotte, drunk and spinning, saying, "Girls, I've known you all my life. What would I do without you, girls?" How bittersweet it is, when she says that. How she wonders what it would be like to be nineteen again, or twenty-one. But she'll settle for this, curled up with her friends in front of the fire. When they arrive in Vancouver, her life will return to normal. Heading home to Saskatoon again, catching up on all the time she's missed.

You're afraid of why it comes to you, clear as a picture. You tell yourself you're bound to Charlotte, but what you're afraid of is this: instead of getting on with your life, you're following her. To make sure that she's gone. To chase her out of your life. In all these vivid imaginings, you are the spectator, the watcher, the one who refuses to leave until the last act. You move through your emotions, anger settling on you like some forgotten weight. It makes you watch until the end.

So badly, you want to be the person who grieves for her. Not the envious one, the one whose heart has toughened up. You're standing on the road. There's even a space for you. A bus stop, of sorts, lit up with harsh fluorescent lights. You never stray from it. No matter what, come hell or high water, come death or disease, you'll stand there watching it all unfold.

When you see the accident, you know it must have happened a hundred times before. The stretch of highway heading to Lloydminster, straight as an arrow. Wide open, it tricks the driver into believing she's awake.

You almost convince yourself you're there, that it's you, semi-conscious in the driver's seat: exactly when you realize that the car is out of control, that it cannot be undone, exactly when, you're not sure. Even the impact seems part of your dream. It knocks you out. But not before you see Charlotte, sitting beside you, the slow-motion crumbling of the passenger side. Her sleeping body, belted in, thrown sideways. She's in your lap, slouched awkwardly against your body. You know you're going under. The car. You have the sensation the car is closing in. Then you don't even know it, you're under, the three of you in your seats.

Later on, Heather can only say, *We were speeding and the car slipped out of control.* Hundred and forty kilometers on a flat stretch of highway. Over the ditch and straight for a tree on the border of a farmhouse.

When the crash comes, this is what you see: lights flashing on all around. Houses you couldn't see for the dark. Snapping to life. Hurrying out into road, all these people, half-dressed. Running in the dewy grass.

The car is wrapped around the tree, the interior light miraculously blinking.

You don't want to be lovesick. You dream yourself sitting in an orange rocking chair, a steaming cup of coffee resting on the arm, the chair tipping back and forth and nothing spills. As if you could do that.

Keep moving and the tiny thing you balance, the thing that threatens, stays secure. You love your husband, love him in a way that makes you heartsick. You think it is irrational to feel this way, to be so overwhelmed by the small tragedies of your life when all around you, there are images of men and women and children, in Dili there are the ones who never ran away to hide in the mountains. You pray for them in the best way you know how. You picture them standing on the street on a summer day, dust against their feet. You picture them safe. Before you know it, your hands are clasped in front of your face. It takes you aback, the way you sit there, shocked and unhappy.

Hardly a month passed between the time you found the letters and the night the accident happened. In the morning, your husband heard the news by phone. He stayed on the phone all morning, calling one person then another. He knew them all, Jean and Heather and Charlotte, childhood friends from Saskatoon. You learned that after the car hit the tree, Jean and Heather stood up and walked away. In shock, Heather started running, straight down the road. An elderly man, still dressed in pajamas, guided her gently back to the site.

It was Heather who called your husband. "Charlotte was asleep the whole time," she told him. "She never felt a thing."

If your husband grieved, he did the gracious thing

and refused to show it. When you asked him how he felt, he held himself together. "I don't know," he said. "It's over."

The expression on his face was closed and you knew better than to push. You left him alone in the apartment. It's space that he needs and that's what you give him. No confrontation or rehashing of that small betrayal, though each day you tilt between anger and sorrow. You expect his grief, are willing to understand it even. Still, he refuses to part with it — his private sorrow is not on display for you. It belongs to him alone.

These days, he spends hours reading the paper. But you can tell that it's only a cover. Like you, he's thinking. Your house is a silent place. The two of you, solicitous but lost in thought, the radio constantly murmuring in the living room. And because you believe in protocol, in politeness and respect, you don't ask him and you never mention her name. When you dropped those letters into the trash, you were telling him the terms of your agreement. Don't mention it, you were saying. Pretend it never happened. Both of you like two cedars, side by side and solitary.

You'd never met Charlotte. You worry that it's sick, this fascination with her life. But in the middle of the day, your hands poised over the keyboard, you have a vivid image of her in the passenger seat, asleep and dreaming. Something in you wants to reach your hand out, the way children lay their fingers on the television screen. When the car leaves the road, you want to nudge it back. Point it back on course. Let it not end like this.

Really, you are just a bystander. It's your husband who should be there, standing in the road. You in the background, curious. It's your husband whose emotions run deep, who weeps the way he never did in real life. If this were a picture, you would be a blur in the background.

Saskatchewan is a photo to you, a duotone of blue and gold. Wheat fields bent against the wind or motionless in the heat, a freeze frame. There's a picture of Charlotte when she was sixteen, a lovely girl standing outside of a barn laughing, dark hair shaking against the blue sky. You have never been to Saskatchewan. Imagine a sky so huge it overwhelms you. Wheat vast as the desert. You picture Charlotte on a dirt road somewhere, a road that cuts through a field. This is the way that you remember her, because between you and your husband, she will always have a kind of immortality.

For a long time you think of her as the kind of person you would like to be. She is a farmer's daughter, a one-time schoolteacher, a bus driver. You think of her as a dreamer. People are drawn to her. They say, *She really knows how to live.* Even you, in your make-believe world, are drawn to her. You watch the way her hands move, not gingerly, not tentatively. You hear her voice. It booms through space.

You play a game with her. The kind of game friends play to pass the time. *If I was an animal, what kind of animal would I be?* You tell her she is an elephant, a tiger, a gazelle. Your husband, she says, is a camel. He is a long-haul kind of man. But what are you? A tern, she says. You do not know what this is. A bird, she says. It flies over the sea. It is swift in flight. You imagine it is the kind of bird that could fly forever. Given the choice, it would never land. You say this is a fault and she laughs. She says you see the negative in everything. She has a smile that fills the room. What kind of person are you? There's some part of you that's glad she's gone. Glad that all those qualities, that smile, that confidence, couldn't save her.

You make a list of all the things you're afraid of: Nuclear catastrophe. Childbirth. War. A failed marriage. As if there is any equality between these things. You know that writing them out will not make them go away. But the list worries you. You don't want to be selfish. Walking along your Vancouver street, you press a blueberry muffin into the hand of a young man sitting on the sidewalk beside his dog.

There's an apple in your coat pocket you're saving for someone else.

At home, you and your husband lie beside each other in bed, sunlight streaking through the blinds. You lie motionless like people in shock. A part of you knows that you're doing everything wrong. You know it, but still, you're sitting at the kitchen table each day, working hard. While researching Japanese glass floats, you come across the *ama* — divers in Japan's coral reefs who, with neither wetsuits nor oxygen masks, search the water for abalone. For up to two minutes at a time, these women hold their breath underwater. Their lung capacity astonishes you. Some of the *ama* are as old as sixty. Imagine them dotting the water, chests bursting for air, going on about their daily work.

One night, when neither of you can sleep, you take a late-night walk together. Through sidewalks coated with autumn leaves, you walk hand-in-hand. It is three in the morning and the streets are empty. A car turning the corner sweeps its lights across you, then disappears. You can hear it travelling away from you, you listen until the sound evaporates. At one point, in a gesture that reminds you of children, your husband swings your hand back and forth, and your joined arms move lightly between you.

The road you are following goes uphill, ending in

a circle of mansions. There is a small green park in the center and this is where you and your husband stop, turning slowly, examining the houses, trying to guess if the mansions are really abandoned as they appear. Nothing stirs. Out here, in this dark patch of land, it's easy to believe that only you and he exist. In the quiet, your husband hums softly, a tune you can't identify. He catches your eye and stops abruptly. You look at him with so much grief and anger, it surprises you both, what you can no longer withhold.

He tells you that it is unforgivable, what he has done. But he cannot go back and he does not know how to change it.

Something in your body collapses. It just gives way. Maybe it is the expression on your husband's face, telling you that there is no longer any way out. You tell your husband you've been seeing strange things, imagining cities you've never visited, people you've never met. You say, "I cannot go on like this any more," and your own words surprise you, the sad certainty of them.

He paces behind you, nodding his head, then begins walking the perimeter of the park. As he walks away from you, your husband raises his voice, as if he believes that no one can hear him. Perhaps he no longer cares if anyone does. He tells you more than you can bear to hear. He says that when he read Charlotte's letter, he was devastated. He wished her so far away that he would never see her again. He talks and he cannot stop. He says he is afraid of being alone, afraid of making terrible mistakes. He is ashamed of being afraid.

This is what you wanted, finally. Here is his private grief, laid out in view of the world. But your chest is bursting with sadness. You are not the only ones affected. There is still that woman who haunts you. What will she think of all your efforts, your tossing, your fear and guilt? How long will she remain with you?

Out front, the houses are still. You stand on your side of the park, watching for signs of movement, expecting the lights to come on, expecting people to come hurrying into the road.

In the end, you know that the two of you will pick yourselves up, you will walk home together not because it is expected or even because it is right. But because you are both asking to do this, in your own ways, because you have come this far together.

For a long time you stand this way, the two of you hunched in the grass. In your mind's eye there are people all around the world turning, diving, coming up for air. Your husband and you in this quiet circle. He crouches down to the ground, face in his hands. There is Charlotte, asleep and dreaming in a car moving through the Prairies. Your husband comes to his feet and looks for you, through the dark and the trees. One perilous crossing after another.

House

——————————————————— ¤ ¤ ¤

It is Kathleen's idea to go back to the house. She knows the bus route, a number 16 up to 49th Avenue, then east to the dividing line where Vancouver rolls into suburb. Lorraine, who is ten years old, is only following along, keeping her older sister company.

At the bus stop, Kathleen fishes coins from her purse. When the bus pulls up and swings its doors open, they hurry up the stairs. Outside, the city blurs by until the neighborhood changes, the streets and shops suddenly familiar. Passing the flower shop on Knight Street, Lorraine has a sudden vision of her mother standing, on the sidewalk there, her hands roaming the plants, her face lit up by the bloom of color. Kathleen rings the bell for the stop and they climb down. Half a block away from the main road, their old house comes into view.

Lorraine barely recognizes it. She stops on the grass out front and tries to imagine herself sitting in the front window. She can almost see her mother there, sitting on the steps, straight hair blowing loose across her face. She imagines her father's white pickup turning in the driveway, her father running up the stairs and disappearing into the house. Lorraine watches the windows for signs of movement, but there is none. It is the third Friday in September, and they have come all the way across the city to visit their old house and mark their mother's birthday.

The two girls pace the sidewalk out front. More than a year has passed since they lived here. Kathleen pauses, admiring the flowers. The lawn is cropped nice and short and they're careful not to walk on it.

"Let's wait over there," Kathleen says, "and see if she comes." They walk across the street. While Lorraine sits heavily down on the curb, Kathleen kicks her sandals off. She hops up and down on the dry grass, glowing with anticipation.

Lorraine tries not to think about school, or about what Liza, their Foster Mom, will say. Instead, she examines every house in turn to pass the time. Red-shingled roof over here and, next door, deep-green curtains pulled tight. Lorraine knows now what her mother meant when she told their father, "Without you, I fall apart." She knows what the words would mean, *I miss you.* The word *miss* encapsulates everything.

Her mother has three pale circles on her left arm, scars from an inoculation she'd had as a child. Lorraine once lifted the sleeve of her father's shirt and found the same three exact markings. She pictured her mother and father as long-lost twins, sailing down the birth canal joined at the upper arm, pulled apart, the marks ballooning inward like buttonholes. Lately all Lorraine thinks about is her mother: her shoes on the sidewalk clipping along, her muddy-blond hair cut short and left to grow out slowly over months and months until it feathered up against her shoulder blades. When she was little, Lorraine thought her mother's hair was directly related to the passing of time, short in the summer, long in winter, in-between in all the other seasons.

Mom and Dad, sometimes together, sometimes apart, are lodged in Lorraine's head. Try as she might, Lorraine can't make them leave. She thinks she shouldn't try. If they disappear, she doesn't trust herself to bring them back again.

Before she left, her mother used to sing in the church choir. Sometimes she brought them upstairs with her and they'd sit behind the pipe organ. The adult voices folded and hung in the alcove. Her mother's voice rang out, blissful. After church, they'd walk to the car and, if her dad was in the city, they'd pile into his white pickup and go for brunch at Mother Tucker's. In summer, the strawberries on the fruit buffet were bigger than Lorraine's fist. Once, her mother took a strawberry and sunk it in her beer glass, laughing. When she lifted it out, it spun gold and sharp. Her mother laughed so hard she knocked the glass over and ruined everything, her father's omelette, Kathleen's French toast. Lorraine couldn't stop laughing. The way her mother's face scrunched up and her eyes watered and her hair came down tangled from its elastic band, Lorraine laughed along with her. Even when she saw her father's face, she couldn't stop. In the car on the way home, her father drove so fast everything blurred, her mother singing out the car window, into the hot breeze.

The morning her mother left, Lorraine climbed into her parents' bed and sniffed their scents on the pillows. Eyes shut, she walked into their closet, dresses and shirts waving together as she moved from side to side. She thought about sleeping there, folded among the clothes, waking in a hundred years when her parents beat the door down and kissed her awake and told her what she knew all along, that this was the bad dream.

Instead, her older sister Kathleen came and flung the closet doors open and pulled her out. Pulled her right into her arms and kept her there. Kathleen, who used to take care of their mother, turned all her love on Lorraine. She kissed her hair and Lorraine felt it all come together, what was real and what was not. As if she had been plunged up into the cold air, clear as day.

Lorraine remembers lying face-down in the middle of an intersection last year. She was nine years old and screaming hysterically. Her mother gripped Lorraine's hands, begging and crying, and tried to drag her up, but Lorraine pawed at the ground. Cars swerved around them, horns blaring. Lorraine had the sensation that she was dying. She was blind and everything was wet. The world was ending here in the road, red leaves muddied on the concrete, people striding past, exhaust thick in her mouth. Her mother, webs of blood vessels bursting in her cheeks, kneeling on the concrete. Then, somehow, the two of them were standing on the curb, Lorraine tipped over against her mother, the two of them sobbing uncontrollably.

At home, her mom drank until her eyes were bulging. She lay down in bed and Lorraine watched the sheet float up, float down with her breath. Lorraine climbed into bed beside her and held on, one arm circling her mother's rib cage.

"We're a pair," her mother said, words running together. "How do you like that? The pair of us."

Lorraine stared at her mother's slender hands, the nails soft and ragged. "I like it that we are a pair," she whispered.

Her mom shook her head. "No," she said. "Wrong answer."

Late that night, her father called from Port Hardy where he was logging the Island. He always called her mother *darling*, cajoling her until she blushed and giggled. "Jesus, I miss you," she said, half crying into the receiver. "I can't hold it together without you." Then she went up to bed, her face wrecked.

"I hear you threw a tantrum," he said, when it was Lorraine's turn to talk to him.

She nodded her head against the phone. "I did." Lorraine didn't know how to explain her actions. She only knew that once she had laid herself down on the concrete, she no longer wanted to stand up again.

Her father waited. Lorraine imagined the phone cord tangling away into nighttime, her father's big shoulders curved forward. "Don't we have enough money?" she asked.

"Of course we do." Her father laughed cheerfully. "What do you want to buy?"

"Nothing."

"Is that why you kicked up a fuss?" he teased.

"If we have enough money, why do you have to live there?"

He was quiet for a moment. Then he said, "I'll be back soon enough. By Christmas, with so many presents you won't know what to do with them."

She heard her dad smoking, the exhalation long into his throat. "Hey," he said. "Don't believe everything your mother says."

"Like what?"

"Oh well," he sighed, "sometimes she flies off the handle."

Lorraine wanted to shake the phone. "She's drunk all the time."

"All the time!" he hooted. "You should have seen her when she was young."

Summer was the longest season. It was the time when all the trees came down, felled by her father before the winter frost set in. They wouldn't see him for months. He might call, homesick from the camps. He promised to bring them up there one day. They could watch the log lines, trees hoisted down the mountain, air full of sawdust. He promised he would get a job in the city next year. Those times when her mother believed him, she gathered them up and put *Blue* in the CD player. Her mother loved to dance. She danced with the girls, ice cubes clinking in her glass. Their mother, the fun-time girl, with her short summer hair. Her pale white arms gone soft.

When she didn't believe him, she'd lie in bed and sleep. She'd take her purse and say, "I'll be home in an hour," and she wouldn't be home again until the night of the second day.

A weekday on a residential street is full of ritual. Sprinklers hum back and forth, pattering the sidewalk. Small children bask in wading pools, laughing their bubbling laughter; the occasional phone is ringing and ringing. Lorraine and Kathleen pace the sidewalk. Halfway down, there's a sprinkler blocking their path, the water arcing over the concrete to hit road and a fringe of grass. Kathleen scowls. "See that? That shouldn't be allowed. It's *waste*." She walks around the arc of water, prim and proper, stepping out onto the silent baking street. Lorraine goes straight through, the water speckling her clothes and skin. She blinks in the coolness of it and keeps on along the sidewalk.

The midday sun burns down relentlessly. They sit in the shade of a mailbox, heels bouncing up and down on the curb. Lorraine sits with Kathleen's head cradled in her lap. She absently rolls a strand of her sister's hair round and round her pinkie until Kathleen tells her it hurts. Lorraine lies back and watches the sky shift slowly above them, but her sister can't sit still. She scans the street, excited, happier than Lorraine has seen her in a long time. She gets up and sprints to the corner store, and when she comes back, her hands are full of goodies — a plastic bag of sour keys and two cans of pop. They eat the candy meticulously, one bite at a time. They work up a sweat chewing. When they're done, they throw the cans and wrappers down, watch them roll off the curb.

Kathleen lies back on the grass, legs tucked against her chest. "No one owns this grass," she says suddenly. "All this stuff between the sidewalk and the curb? It's no one's. So it's mine." She gets comfortable on it, sprawls out luxuriously, her shorts riding high on her thighs.

A young woman in pumps steps past them on the sidewalk. She dangles a letter from her fingers and Kathleen dutifully rolls over to let her pass. The woman drops her letter into the mail slot, then glances at them impatiently. "What are you girls doing sitting around on a school day?"

"It's none of your business," Kathleen says, "but we're waiting for our mom."

The woman frowns. "You shouldn't be sitting in the sun," she says, sternly. "Didn't your mother teach you that?"

Kathleen watches the woman walk away. "I said it was none of your business, anyway," she mutters.

But Lorraine is watching the house. A woman is in the window now, peering out at them as she talks on the phone. Her hand twirls the cord, reaches up to hold the bottom of the receiver, her head falling forward, nodding. Then she turns away from them, back to the room, and then she is gone.

Kathleen stares at the empty window, then shifts closer to Lorraine. "I'd bet money on it," she says, her face flushed. "Any minute now, Mom will come walking up the street."

Lorraine has no answer to this. She remembers something her dad said once. "It's a kind of love," he told them. "The way she drank. It was like being in love."

On her own birthday last year, their mother took them to Cipriano's. She never drank like other people, in celebration. On her birthday she stayed sober. Twenty-four hours every year, just to prove that she could. The restaurant was small and hot, and they ate wedges of garlic bread and drank Shirley Temples and Luke Skywalkers. There were paper umbrellas tucked in the drinks. Lorraine loved her mom's face in candlelight, the way her hair fell straight as a turning page. They ate pasta from heaping plates, mounds of spaghetti topped with red, crumbly meatballs. They lingered over hot chocolate. Lorraine and Kathleen tried not to notice how their mother watched wine being poured at another table, how it stole her attention.

They said things to distract her but it was over too soon. Their mother paid the bill and they left, but there were no doors, just a wide rectangular window that you stepped through into the humid evening.

Lorraine wanted to make it to fourteen. When she was fourteen, like her sister, she would have all this sorted out. Like Kathleen, she would believe that their mother would come back for them. She would be able to divide her mom's sickness from her mom's real self and she would keep them separate like glasses of water.

Back then, she couldn't decipher when her mother was telling the truth. It changed from moment to moment, fluctuating like an off-kilter heart. Those times when her mother emerged from the bedroom, eyes lit up and dancing, Lorraine knew she shouldn't trust her. This was her mother full of lies, the one who'd walk away and forget them.

"This thing that I do," she told them once, "it does so much more good than harm."

Then she combed her hair straight back off her face so she looked like a movie star, her blue eyes like saucers, and drove to the store. Later on, after she had drunk the house empty, she lay on the sofa and wept, said, "What have I done? Ten years. I just blew it all." Lorraine never knew what to say. That night she dreamed her mother was laughing, a swooping sound that reminded Lorraine of a seagull hoisted on the wind, dropping fast. She dreamed her mother died. All morning she believed it was true, until her mother pulled up in the driveway and ran into the house, the car still running and the door wide open, her mother swaggering heroically on the stairs.

The morning her mother left, Lorraine was standing on the lawn. Kathleen had mowed it once, months ago. The grass was knee-high now, maybe higher. She and Kathleen used to stand in the grass blowing dandelion spores to the four winds. Now the yard bloomed with them.

Her mother walked out carrying her purse in her hands like a loaf of bread, her fingers curled around the bottom. She was wearing her coat even though the sky was cloudless and heat blared down. Lorraine sat camouflaged in the grass. She watched her mother's progress along the walk, one foot steady in front of the other. The sun on the back of her mother's hair turned it blond. That hair, the prettiness of it, made Lorraine think there was nothing wrong. Not in the way her mother walked or the direction she went or her purse in her hands like a gift. She watched her mother and it might have been any day of the year, neither here nor there, a nothing picture. Her mother walked away down the street, turned left, and disappeared.

Three nights passed. She and Kathleen stayed up late watching old movies on the television. "I'm not worried," Kathleen said. "Are you?" Lorraine shook her head.

It terrified Lorraine to wake up in the morning. She was used to finding her mother around the house, sometimes on the floor, right beside Lorraine's bed. Her mother's mouth would be fully open, churning the air in and out, a lone swimmer.

On the fourth day, they called their father. Long distance, the telephone lines snaking across the water and up into the Island's northern tip. Lorraine tried to calm herself by picturing him, phone cradled against his shoulder, mountains and forest in the background. He asked them over and over, "But when did you last see her?"

"Days ago, days ago, days ago."

"What did she say?"

"She didn't say anything."

"I promise you," he told them. "She'll be back before I make it home."

They wandered around the empty house eating peanut-butter sandwiches. Kathleen stared out the front window. "Mom's coming back today," she said. "She doesn't know what to do without me." Lorraine's head hurt. She went and stood inside her mother's closet, wondering if they would be able to take it with them when they left the house.

The next day, when her father walked in the door, Lorraine was lying on the carpet, her hand pressed to the cave of her stomach. Kathleen came out of the bedroom hysterical. She was screaming and it was so out of character that Lorraine sat up, her brain muddy. It looked like Kathleen and her father were dancing, the way his hands clamored around her shoulders, then her head. If only it were quieter. She lay still thinking that if everyone would leave her alone, she might be able to get up off the floor and find her way into bed. Then she became afraid that she was not real at all. In this room was Kathleen, unable to breathe, sobbing. Her father, calming her with his sad voice. And then the nothing of herself like a crumb in the carpet, gradually becoming nothing at all.

Lorraine remembers that after their mother left, they went up to the logging camps with their father. They drove for hours along gravel roads. In the geographical center of the Island, the trees opened up into a little town. The air was so clean it hurt Lorraine's throat. She tilted her head to the sky and the trees pointed up forever. Their father took them up to the side of a mountain where boys as young as twenty were taking the trees down one by one.

"You see," her dad said, as they drove along the logging roads, "I never could have brought you here." He was wearing a white T-shirt, suspenders, and jeans. His skin was dark and shining from the sun. "This isn't any place for a family. No shopping malls, no movies, nothing to do."

Lorraine didn't bother to argue. They watched from the car while sunset turned the sky a blistering orange.

There was a general store in the camp, the kind that sold milk and cheese among the diapers and saws. Her father towered over the shelves, his big hands scooping up Popsicles from the freezer and packages of marshmallows. Outside the tent, when the night was pitch black but the air was still warm, they sang songs around the campfire. Kathleen had a voice like an angel, thick and rolling like their mother's. "Boy," Dad said, his voice scratchy, "you sure know how to raise the dead, don't you?"

When he lay back in the dirt and his face disappeared in the darkness, he told them how excited their mother had been when she first found out she was pregnant. She thought it would turn her life around. Their father shrugged his shoulders. "She thought I might give up this kind of life. Move back to the city. Don't ever think it's your fault, because the one to blame is sitting right here. I was no help to her. I kept

telling her I had my work. I had all this work to do."
His voice was dry as sand.

When they got back to the city, their father arranged everything. He took them to meet their social worker. He explained that he wasn't up to raising a family, that he'd had his chance and lost it. Kathleen, distant and aloof, told him, "We'll be fine. Don't change your plans on our account." Lorraine said nothing. She couldn't bring herself to look at him. Eventually, the social worker found Liza, their new Foster Mom.

On the day he dropped them off at Liza's, he said he'd never forget them. Lorraine said the same and she wasn't lying. Dad, smelling of the great outdoors and cabin sleeping, would never fade. He'd always been a memory. But her mother, with her disheveled blond hair, was already slipping by. When Lorraine tried to recall her face, it seemed to disappear from view.

When her father drove away and left them there, Lorraine knew she would remember it forever — white smoke trailing out the back, his left arm stretched out the window, temporarily fluttering, and the car rolling across the driveway, rolling out of sight.

Lorraine and Kathleen watch an entire day pass in front of their house. By four o'clock, people start coming home from work. They walk quickly down the sidewalk, stepping over Kathleen's bare, out-stretched legs, their eyes averted. Lorraine is slumped against the mailbox, one hand covering her face. Kathleen scans the street, hands on her hips. She catches sight of a truck rounding the corner. It is a white pickup. Lorraine sits up, her heart beating fast.

"Has she come with Dad?" Kathleen says, walking into the road. "Is that her in the truck with Dad?"

In the afternoon sunshine, their father's truck comes floating by, slowing down in front of their house, then speeding up again. Lorraine sits rooted to the sidewalk. The white pickup swims in front of Lorraine's eyes, but she can see right away there is no one in the passenger seat. Kathleen jumps up and down, behind the car, waving her arms, "Stop! Stop! We're right here!" He hits the brakes. Lorraine sees it in slow motion, his head lurching forward then swiveling around, his eyes through the glass, shocked and alarmed.

Kathleen stands awkwardly in the road, hand raised in an adult gesture. Their father stares through the windshield at them, uncomprehending. "Well, well," he says, when he steps out of the truck. He smiles but his face is guarded. "So you've come back to see the old place."

Kathleen doesn't move. She is searching the truck with her eyes.

"House is falling apart, isn't it? We got out just in time."

A car, pulling out of a driveway, swerves carefully around them.

"It's a joke," her father says, his voice low. "Kathleen, I'm joking."

She nods her head, still looking past him. "We're out of money," she blurts out. "Couldn't even buy an ice-cream cone."

Lorraine stares at their feet on the sidewalk.

"It's Mom's birthday, you know?" Kathleen laughs nervously. "It's so hard waiting. She won't drink at all today. I just want her to hurry up and come."

Their father looks at her, then out across the street, at the two-story house. He takes Kathleen's hand. Together, they walk over to where Lorraine is sitting. Lorraine's never seen him so dressed up, a tweed jacket and gray slacks. His face, sunburnt and dry, is dark in the sunlight. When he crouches down and brings his hand to Lorraine's face, she can see the lines of dirt in his palm, grainy and deep. "How are things with Liza?" he asks her.

"They're fine."

"Liza cooks good food," Kathleen says. She lifts her pinkie to her mouth, chews a bit of skin, then nods. "She doesn't know we're here."

"We should call home then. Let her know you're

safe." A string of cars grumbles past. He looks over at them. "Must be almost a year now since I've seen you two. You're all grown up." He scuffs his shoes against the curb, looks at his watch, then sits down. "I don't get out to the city much any more. If I get some time off work, I take the ferry across. I drive by the old place, just to make sure it's still standing up."

"Tell us you can't stay away," Kathleen says. Her voice sounds distant and mocking. She plucks a handful of grass from the dirt.

He laughs, embarrassed. "Can't stand to see it and I can't stand not to."

Lorraine pulls her knees up to her chest and leans back against the mailbox. Kathleen scatters grass on her own bare skin.

"There's a woman inside," Kathleen tells their father, pointing at the house. "We saw her blabbing on the phone."

"Her husband bought the house. Scooped it up. He's a doctor or something." He stands, smoothing his pants with both hands, then strides quickly across the street and gives the house a once-over. "I don't like those flowers," he says when he comes back. "Rhododendrons. They're as common as rain."

"Mom liked them," Kathleen says.

He looks at her, then crosses his arms across his body as if shielding himself.

"She used to stand out there, beside the flowers."

"Yes," he says. "I remember that. She had a soft spot for them."

"I used to cut them for her and put them in the kitchen when she wasn't feeling well. I bet you didn't know that."

He shakes his head. After a moment, he says, "I'm glad you did that."

Kathleen doesn't respond.

Their father sits down beside them on the curb. "I know it's her birthday today. She never was one to celebrate." He nods at the house. "There's your lady again." The blond woman is back at the window, setting the table. A man and a child are sitting down to dinner.

Kathleen leans forward, eyes fixed on them.

Passing cars blow dust off the road. Their father starts to say something, lifting his hand, but then he stops. He spreads his fingers on the curb, his eyes unreadable, and looks up again through the picture window.

Once, not long after they came to live with Liza, Lorraine woke up to find Kathleen next to her in the bottom bunk, their arms wrapped around each other like long-lost relatives. Lorraine lay still and tried not to breathe. She couldn't understand how they ended up like this, tangled together. She prodded Kathleen awake to ask her. Kathleen scrunched her eyebrows, as if she were trying to remember too.

"You were dreaming," Kathleen finally said. "You were dreaming and saying funny things."

"What things?"

"You were tossing and turning and calling for Mom."

"No. I wasn't."

Kathleen shrugged. She loosened her grip around Lorraine's stomach. "You don't have to believe me. I was only trying to help."

Lorraine took a deep breath. She told Kathleen what she thought. "Mom's dead."

"Don't be stupid," Kathleen snapped. "You'll make it true if you believe that."

Three days ago, Kathleen woke up choking and wheezing, her eyes wet with tears. Lorraine stood and reached for her. Then Liza was there, her hands on Kathleen's slippery back. She rocked her and Kathleen said, "Go away," over and over again, even while she held Liza's wrists, the pressure of her fingers turning Liza's skin white. "Go away," she whispered, but the words didn't mean anything. They floated up in the room, above where Liza and Kathleen hunched tangled together in the top bunk, their heads brushing the ceiling. And Lorraine down on the floor with her hands reaching up, thinking words didn't mean anything, and least of all what they said. These were words: *alcoholic, trauma.* But they never linked up to her life. Only her mother's loose smile, her damaged face, her purse in her hands. Lorraine remembers a windstorm on a hot June night. They watched it from inside, turning the city dusty when the electricity went off. She remembers looking at her mother's mouth, the lips chapped and dry, how they opened to say something, about the storm, about anything, but no words came out. On the lawn, the trees swayed forward, leaning to the east.

Out on the sidewalk, the three of them have not spoken for a long while, and the sun is beginning to set. The street is quiet and a chill wind rustles the trees. Her father looks from them to the house and back again. His voice is low when he says, "I think I understand why you're here, and I have no right to say it, but I don't think she's coming back."

Kathleen lifts her head to look at her father. Then she turns her face away, as if that will stop her from hearing.

"Christ knows, I can't stop thinking about her either." He takes his hands and folds them together, holding them in his lap as if they might jump away.

"I'm the same as you. I want her to come back. Maybe she will, sooner or later." He looks at Kathleen's expression. "Maybe today, even," he says gently. He settles back against the mailbox, his shoulders sagging. "We drank too, out in the bush. Maybe your mother would have liked that life. But I wanted her to get clean, to pull herself together. I never counted on her leaving. I never thought she'd do it."

He stares across at the house, at a loss for words. Now or never, sooner or later, Lorraine thinks. Still, she looks at the crest of the street. A woman walking towards her, she can see it in her mind's eye. She can see the four of them embracing in the road and how they cry, but it isn't like crying at all. It's something else. She looks at her sister. Beside their father, Kathleen's face is buried in her knees.

Lorraine's father has his arms around them. He is sitting beside Kathleen, and his arm reaches past her to brush Lorraine's shoulders with his fingers. Kathleen is crying now. She's saying, "I let her go. I saw her walking. I *knew*. I knew she was going."

Her father says, "Shh. Shhh."

"Everybody blames me," she tells him.

"Nobody does."

Her hands are covering her face and tears are flowing out of her hands. "Don't you blame me?" she asks Lorraine.

"No," Lorraine says. "I never have."

Their father turns his head again and again as if to clear it. "I can't save you," he says. "I can't do it."

Lorraine looks into his face. "I know," she says.

Kathleen's eyes are wild and sad. They dart from her to the street and the house and back again. The street goes forever. Their father leaves his arm around her, like a last line, to pull them back again.

They waited until it was dark and then their father drove them home. The sky was very clear. On the other side of the city, there were celebrations. There were hundreds of thousands of people gathered on the shoreline watching fireworks. How they blazed up from a floating raft, burst in the sky, and rained down. From the car, Lorraine couldn't see them but she could hear the explosions. They came every few seconds, like approaching artillery. Their father drove slowly, taking side streets and alleyways, watching for pedestrians. Kathleen watched with him. They drove in silence, peering up at the fireworks. Lorraine refused to look. In her mind's eye, she was watching a woman in a long coat, too warm for this summer night. The woman was standing in front of the house like someone in mourning. She was admiring the flowers and thinking of her children and husband. There was that windstorm, remember? Trees leaning to the east. They were bending and she felt like she was running among them. They were calling for her; so many things did. She drank to stop her grief. But when she stood in front of this house, she pictured her children and her husband, she pictured how they climbed into his truck together, how he comforted them, so that when they left, when they turned their backs on the house, all their grief was left behind. The picture went on and on. She would never leave. She was alighting from a bus. She was standing on the corner waiting for the light to change. The truck sped on the empty streets, and she was still there.

Bullet Train

Harold

When Harold was a boy, he drowned his sorrow by flying kites. In the mornings, he pedaled his bike out along the residential streets where the winter drizzle made the asphalt shine. He biked under the streetlamps, through the rain puddles, all the way to the lake. On the grass, he slid off and left the bike lying on its side, the front wheel still spinning.

Harold unraveled the line. He ran and looked backwards. He was good at keeping it up, good at angling it over the lake. The kite shouldered left then straightened out. Harold put some slack on the line, then pulled it taut. And all the time he thought about the rain, or when the lake would freeze over, or how his mother kept spare change in a red metal box. He wondered how far down in the ocean he'd have to swim to see phosphorescence with his own two eyes. He could swim forever, he thought. From this side of Trout Lake to the other, and back again. His dad was a fine swimmer too; he always mentioned how he used to swim competitively, back in his university days. But that was long ago, too long to count. Donkey's years, his dad would say.

After half an hour, he let the kite down, watched it fall in slow motion to the lake. Then he reeled it in fast, just like fishing. Watched it tear across the surface of the water. Right until it bumped against Harold's shoes. He gathered it up and held it in his arms, the bright yellow fabric still damp.

On the way home, he dodged between cars, pedaling so fast little droplets of water shot off the handlebars and off the wet tires. Right up the alley to the front door, where he dropped his bike in the grass and pounded up the steps, the kite in his hands, right into the coffee-smelling kitchen and his dad's Famous Breakfast. Famous, his dad said, because it was as dull as dull could be. Two pieces of toast each, and a bowl of lumpy oatmeal.

His dad leaned down to pat his head and then they sat across the table from each other, gulping breakfast down before his dad hurried out the door and off to work.

Harold was nine years old and he felt he was living life on his tiptoes. One morning, he crept downstairs to put the coffee on. He tried to move as softly as he could past his mother's bedroom. The door was slightly ajar and he could see the narrow outline of her body beneath the blankets. In the kitchen, he stepped over his dad, who was lying on his back, head and torso under the sink, taking the pipes apart. Harold made coffee and his dad yelled out, "Don't make it so damn weak this time!"

And Harold thought of his grandmother, her soft, wrinkled arms and watery eyes. He thought of snow falling on Trout Lake, how it melted on the surface of the water. He thought of elephants in the *National Geographic*, their sad, baggy eyes.

"Get me a glass of water, will you?" His dad's voice echoed from underneath the sink.

Harold walked to the bathroom and turned on the tap. He thought of dream-catchers, the netting and the beads woven together, holding his most secret wishes.

Sooner or later on the weekends, his father would make him climb the ladder onto the roof. It was a kind of punishment. If Harold forgot to put away the dishes in the dish rack, or if he fell asleep on the couch, as he often did in the afternoons, his dad would lose his temper. He would point his hand towards the roof. "Go think about things. Go sit where I can't see you."

This morning, a Saturday, Harold had forgotten to buy milk for the coffee. When his father asked for the money back, Harold couldn't find it. His father pulled him by the arm onto the back lawn and shoved him up the wooden ladder onto the rooftop. Harold was afraid of heights. He was too terrified to stand so he crouched on all fours. Down below, he could see the neighborhood boys flocking to the back alley, circling the house on their bikes. They turned wheelies in the soft gravel road. "Hey, Harold! You stuck up on the roof again? Can't get down, can you?" They laughed, tilting their bikes up, hopping them gracefully on the back tires. "Hey, when can I go up on the roof? Is it my turn yet?"

Harold's father, weeding the garden, laughed out loud. "Only Harold," he told them, crouched down, his hands full of soil. "Harold's the one who doesn't want to be there."

Harold looked out over the back lawn, at the solid figure of his father pulling up the ground. Nine years old, and all his life he'd been afraid of heights. What he wanted more than anything was to ride his bike up and down the alley, to stand side-by-side in the yard with his father, their four hands full of weeds. On his stomach, he straddled the roof, cheek pressed to the shingles, and thought about the bullet train in Japan, speeding across the country. Cherry blossoms bursting on the street out front. How people described hearts lodged in their throats and he knew that feeling. He missed his mother, missed her like crazy even though she was right there, inside the house. She had a thick braid that swung when she walked. Now, she barely came out of her bedroom at all.

Last week, he had wandered through the house, from room to room, with a pain in his chest. He had gone to his dresser and taken out his clothes, three pairs of pants, a stack of T-shirts, sweaters, socks, and underwear, and laid them in neat piles on the bed. One book, his well-worn encyclopedia. His father came to check on him, and when he saw the piles of clothing, he said, "What's all this for?"

Harold said, "I'm running away."

His father leaned against the door frame.

Harold sat beside his clothes. "These are for me to take. I'll leave the rest in the dresser."

"Will you be gone long?"

Harold nodded.

"I'll tell you what," his father said, clearing a space to sit. "Why don't you give it a few days? See what happens. I think, maybe, things will get better."

Harold sat tight-lipped. His dad turned around to look at the items of clothing. "Why don't you put these back in the drawers for now?" He looked at Harold, his expression pained.

Harold did as he was told. When all the lights went out he lay very still in bed, listening for change. Hoping that by morning, she'd be up and about again.

Now, sitting on the roof, watching the neighborhood boys, he stared down at his father leaning forward into the vegetables. Harold thought of all the chance moments, his mother's car accident, the weakness in her chest, and how she had a cancer there. He always thought that if they let him go free, if he had all the time in the world, he would make himself into a great runner. The kind that ran long marathons, through New York or Chicago, who came to Heartbreak Hill and just kept going. All skin and bones, like his mother said. The kind of boy who, try as he might, could never eat enough to keep himself running.

When it started to rain, Harold's dad climbed up on the ladder. He leaned forward on the rooftop, chin in his hands. "I know you hate it up here," his dad said, "but it will make you stronger. No matter what happens to you from now on, you'll always have this well of strength to draw on."

Will I, Harold thought. He let his father help him down.

In silence, they made ham sandwiches for lunch. Then they carried them into the living room and ate, plates balanced on their knees. He saw the slope of his father's shoulders and the stiffness in his knees, and Harold mirrored it back, curving his spine just so, holding his feet slightly apart. If his mother came down the stairs, she would see the two of them and it would make her laugh. Trying to hide it at first, then letting it burst out. "Look at the both of you," she might say. How he missed her voice. When she walked with him at Trout Lake, when she said to him, "It's the details, you see. Once you get the details right, it will fly all on its own." She adjusted his wrist and looked up high, away to the kite he was pulling in. And she threw rocks in the water. And she said he was doing "fine, just fine." When she died, he would take her red metal box, the one that held her spare change. It was filled to the top and he would always keep it that way, he would never remove a single penny.

When he was ten, Harold experienced what he would come to think of as the turning point of his life. There he was, face-down on the roof. It was months after his mother's funeral. She had told him that nothing would ever be the same again, saying this in a voice that was like her voice if it had been left outside in the cold all night. It wavered and it was exhausted, but she still smiled at him and told him he was going to be a fine man. Harold had nodded his head, afraid to look at her. He had closed his eyes and pictured his mother walking along beside him at Trout Lake, the two of them holding hands. He looked her straight in the face and said, "I will never forget you."

Nothing was the same, except here he was again on the roof. It was summer and he could see the waves of heat. They blurred the ground. Down below, his dad sat on a lawn chair, sipping water from a plastic bottle. The shingles on the roof burned Harold's arms and legs. He felt a wave of sickness passing through his body. He turned over, gingerly, so that he was spreadeagled and facing the sky. An airplane was lowering itself through the clouds. He thought it could see him. It could drop a line and he would catch it, like James Bond. Hold on and swing low across the city. He pictured a flower of skydivers billowing from the plane, the wind pressing their faces into stunned amazement.

Harold turned over and pushed himself up on all fours. He crawled slowly down the slant of the roof. He could no longer see the ground so he kept his eyes on his hands. Nobody was watching him. He crawled backwards, each moment expecting the roof to end. When his body began to slide down, he wasn't afraid. Even when his elbows bruised off the rain gutter and his arms darted away from his body as if he was coming apart, he wasn't afraid. This was the end of it, he thought, all the weight of his body left on the roof and the lightest, strongest part of himself tumbling through the air.

Harold opened his eyes and saw the yard and the house. He heard footsteps in the grass. He sat up and saw people running towards him.

⌷

For most of his life, Harold will be shy with women. After he moves out of his father's house, he will keep to himself, making a living by doing repair work and caretaker jobs. Every night for two decades Harold will do one of three things: read, watch television, or listen to the radio. He will take pleasure in the ritual of his day-to-day tasks. Then one day he'll meet Thea and everything will change.

One day he'll wake up beside her, in their apartment on the seventeenth floor. He'll find his mouth open against her neck and he will remind himself of a small animal, dreaming, feeding. In the bedroom, Thea's daughter Josephine will be listening to music and he'll listen to her heavy steps back and forth to the kitchen. Harold will surprise even himself. He'll think, *I've woken up into a dream. I've dreamt up an entire family.*

At first, when Thea and her daughter argue, as they often do, Harold will try to remain unobtrusive. He will pretend to read a book. One night, he will sneak a glance at them: Thea, tough as nails, Josephine, emotional and sarcastic. Both of them yelling to kingdom come. Slouched on the Chesterfield, he'll feel a pang of regret that he hadn't met Thea fifteen years earlier. Josephine will be the closest thing to his own child he will ever have.

This fight will be worse than the others. Josephine's eyes will be red and swollen. "I hate it, I hate it here."

"What has gotten into you? You hardly know this boy."

"We want to move back east!"

"Over my dead body."

"Let me go," Josephine will say, cradling her body in her arms. "Harold, tell her. You understand. Tell her I want to move to Toronto."

"No! Not with that boy. Listen to me. I know what I'm talking about. I was just as impulsive as you once."

"We want to get married."

"It's ridiculous! The two of you are still children."

"Harold!" Thea's daughter will sink to the floor. "Talk to her. Make her see. He's moving and I have to go with him. Or else I'll die. I can't stand it."

Harold will stand up and walk towards them. He will remember a magician he saw once lying on a bed of nails, how the magician laughed the whole time. He never even shed a drop of blood. Harold will think that he could do that, if he put his mind to it. All the things that once seemed impossible. He will walk towards his wife and daughter and realize how far away he is from the boy who sat sorrowful on the roof. He'll feel a pain in his heart, reach up to touch it, and Thea will walk across the room to him. His body will be so light she'll catch him in her arms. He'll see the look on her face, terrified. Terrified. But not Harold. He will be holding on to her with all his strength.

Thea

When Thea met Harold last year, she was a decade younger than he. Thea worked as an outreach nurse. She drove around in a government van handing out clean needles and condoms and jokingly called herself the Protection Lady. In the van were racks of brochures and pamphlets. She sometimes scribbled notes to Harold on these, grocery lists in the margins of Hep B info sheets.

Thea kept her hair loose, long enough to reach the small of her back. There were fine lines webbing out from the corners of her mouth, streaks of gray in her hair. They radiated from her forehead, single strands that Harold would seek out with his fingers.

"What did you go and do that for?" she asked when Harold plucked one with his thumb and forefinger.

He had a boyish smile. She strung her arms around his waist and they sat on the couch together watching television. They watched *The Price Is Right,* Thea biting her lip nervously while a middle-aged man swung the big wheel. "Go Big Money," Thea said, squeezing Harold's hand. Parked in front of the television, she thought of all her days spent lying on the brown carpet in her parents' basement, watching *Divorce Court* and *Donahue.* When she was sixteen, she used to lie there and plan out the details of her life, what kind of marriage, what kind of children, what kind of person.

Driving with her partner Betty in the outreach van, she kept her eyes on the drug addicts and young girls. The girls seemed to turn old right in front of her. Their skin just dried right out, their hair turned limp. If she were the Pied Piper, she would lead them away from the city, over the Cascade Mountains, down into the idyllic valley. If she hadn't drowned herself in *Donahue* episodes when she was a teenager, would she be here now, working these streets? The very idea made Thea laugh. To think that talk shows had shaped her life. It was so ludicrous yet true.

Early in her relationship with Harold, they had driven down to the docks to watch the longshoremen, the Lego blocks of cargo being loaded deep into the freighters. It was a bright afternoon. Thea told him, "I have an excellent memory. It goes with my line of work, I guess. I remember everything someone tells me. I just pack it down. I've always been good with secrets."

"I don't have any secrets to give you," Harold said.

She nodded her head. After a moment, she asked, "Do you trust me?"

"Yes," he said. His face was tired and he had grown too skinny for his clothes. They hung in creased folds along his sides.

"Good," Thea said, grasping his hand. "Because I'll never, ever forget anything you tell me. I'll always remember. I'll always remember everything you tell me."

Thea came from a good family. Her dad was a lawyer who had a tendency to yell in conversation. "HOW WAS SCHOOL?" he would shout. "DID YOU LEARN ANYTHING AT ALL TODAY?" Her mom, a nurse, curled her body forward as if fearing attack. She whispered to Thea, "Is that lipstick you're wearing? Who gave you lipstick?" Thea yelled at her dad and whispered at her mom. At sixteen, she diagnosed herself as schizophrenic.

"I'm hearing voices," she told her father.

"WHAT?"

"I'm hearing voices." She danced around like a witch. "Boo! Boo! You know, voices."

"RIDICULOUS!"

Her mom puttered around the kitchen, lips puckered in a constant "Shhh."

Thea developed a booming voice. She had to just to make herself heard. Dinner conversation was warfare.

"You wouldn't believe how much I paid for this asparagus —"

"PASS IT OVER!"

"— *per pound.* Isn't the world crazy?"

"Here, Dad. Have them all."

"You won't believe what the supermarket girl said to me —"

"IS THAT THE CHECK-OUT GIRL WITH THE LAZY EYE?"

"She said I should just climb down off my wallet and get in line behind everybody else. Can you believe it?"

"IT JUST ROLLS OUT THE SIDE OF HER HEAD, LIKE SHE'S CRAZY."

"Really. Why, I just stood there with my mouth hanging open."

"CAN'T THEY OPERATE ON SOMETHING LIKE THAT NOWADAYS?"

When she was twelve, Thea asked her mother if she loved Thea's father absolutely. Her mom frowned. "That's a difficult question. Do you want me to answer honestly?"

Thea nodded, bracing herself.

"Feelings come and go," her mom said softly. "Some days I love him more than others. Some days I don't love him at all."

At sixteen, Thea fell in love. It was the first time and she was carried away by it. The man was thirty-one years old. He was a helicopter pilot. All year round he worked for Search and Rescue on Mount Seymour, scanning the ground for missing people. At night, she would sit with him, parked in deserted schoolyards, falling in love in the front seat of his truck, the steering wheel marking patterns on their pale winter skin. After months of this, Thea decided to bring him home. She snuck him through her window and into her bed. She pressed her index finger to his lips, daring him to have sex with her on her adolescent bed. He couldn't resist. Thea didn't know she could be this way, her face shocking into misery and happiness, her hand coming down hard on his bare back, believing that some unknown part of her was breaking off and deserting her. She glimpsed its shadow, its out-of-breath escape, and knew she'd never bring it back again.

When her helicopter pilot fell asleep beside her, Thea made the decision not to wake him. She held on to him, her fingers tracing patterns across his chest and down his leg, then over onto her own bare skin. In the morning, she heard her mother climbing out of bed. She heard the shower come on. With her heart in her throat, she listened to her mother's approaching footsteps. Thea pictured what it would look like, her sixteen-year-old body tangled up with this hairy man. She closed her eyes. The bedroom door swung open. Her mother took a half-step into the room. Thea's heart was deafening. There was a long silence. Then her mother closed the door. Thea listened to her mother's silent retreat down the hallway, and the firm click of her mother's door closing.

She was overcome by joy and disappointment. *See, she wanted to cry, I love him absolutely. It is possible, and I do. I do.* She didn't move. She lay in bed, already missing her mother. Her helicopter pilot, sound asleep and snoring, didn't wake for hours.

Pregnancy never frightened her, even when she packed her suitcase, the same one that had seen her through summer camp and three weeks in Germany. She left her parents' house, the sad, faded carpet and the basement television, and booked herself into a home for unwed mothers.

Her helicopter pilot carried her suitcase. He was melancholy. He talked about looking down from the helicopter into the white-out snow, looking for a glimpse, a colorful jacket, a tarp, a single thread of smoke. And when they spotted it, he zeroed in, the helicopter swaying above the ground like a damaged bird, the missing persons looking skyward, arms lifted. Thea lay in his arms and thought of all the growing she would have to do to keep him happy. She was so young, after all, and now this baby was coming. Life was running away with her. Months ago, she was fumbling through trigonometry, sines and cosines, now she was reading up on baby's first month, she was watching videos of underwater births, midwives, breathing. Some of the other girls in the home had ultrasounds of their babies. Thea held them up to the light, and studied them. This baby was just like her. Coming out of this blurriness, waiting to come out sharp and resolute.

On the day of her ultrasound, Thea waited at the clinic for him to come. He was very late. She did the ultrasound without him. Her baby wrapped its legs around the umbilical cord, and bobbed like a deep-sea diver. She sat on the steps of the clinic afterward, the photo on her knee, untouched. A strong wind might come and blow it free. When it started to rain, she walked home. There were no messages for her taped to the door. She phoned his number, fingers sliding over the rotary dial, but no one picked up. Thea scanned the papers for stories of hikers lost in the mountains. She willed one up there, waiting in silent desperation with his tarp, his fire dissipating into air. Her soon-to-be husband wavering above, *tuttuttut* of the choppers.

One day, she stepped out to stretch her legs. On her return she found a note from him, and a gift. A silver-plated bracelet, something that wouldn't cost more than thirty dollars, the kind of thing you rushed to the mall to get before you hurried to catch a plane on your way out of the city. She held the note to her chest and tried not to miss him. But she remembered everything he had ever said. Every word.

¤

Years later, when Josephine is almost fully grown and Harold has moved into the apartment on the seventeenth floor, Thea will be taken aback by her life. She'll look at her daughter and Harold, her strange and wayward family, and be overcome with fear. She'll think that this is the trouble with having too much. She cannot bear the thought of losing one thing.

One day, Harold will collapse in the living room. Even as she is terrified, even as she catches him in her arms, some part of Thea will be relieved. She will think that if Harold survives this, they will have paid a debt — a debt to unhappiness, a nod to tragedy. In the hospital, she will think, *Just one decade of happiness. Please, whoever you are, just one.*

Standing by his hospital bed, Josie will hold Harold's hand. "You were really scared there, weren't you?" she'll ask.

Thea will nod, afraid to speak.

"You really love him, don't you?"

How Josie will remind Thea of herself — those probing questions, that youthful wisdom. She will steal a look at her daughter. "Absolutely."

"It's funny. You hardly know him."

"What do you mean?"

"It's only been a year. How did you get so attached?"

Her daughter will leave her at a loss for words. That night, Thea will drive through the dark Vancouver streets, out to Trout Lake, where Harold once rode his bike as a boy. Out to Rupert Street, and the house for unwed mothers. She will see the ski runs on Mount Seymour all lit up, and in the foreground, the rows and rows of houses. Late at night, she will park her car in front of the apartment. Fumbling for her keys she will catch a glimpse of a car she recognizes. Inside the car will be Josie. The boy will be reclined against the driver-side door. Josie, pressed up against him, her hands on his neck. Thea will feel her heart stop. She will step off the sidewalk, into the bushes. From behind the row of trees, she will stand and watch them.

Thea will remember holding Josie for the first time. Josie was red and scrawny, with a full head of thick, brown hair. One eye was open just a crack. Her hair was tousled and wet. Thea had hugged the bundle to her chest, weeping, not because she saw Josie's father in Josie's sad, scrunched-up face. But because Thea realized that in all her mistakes, in all the failures and missteps, she had finally managed to do something supremely well. Before that moment, she had never understood it was truly possible. Thea will stand on the grass, leaning against a tree. Inside the car, Josie will slip her T-shirt off. Thea will stare up at the rooftops. She will rest for a while standing there. Then she will catch her breath and head inside.

Josephine

It was a clear night. Josephine and her mother sat on the balcony drinking fruit punch, looking out over the expanse of houses and industrial docks. They could see as far as the sulphur hills and the double strand of lights along the Lions Gate Bridge. Inside the apartment, Harold watched *Jeopardy!*, shouting out the answers.

Josie sipped her punch. She had never been afraid of heights. Even as a child, she used to come out here and pitch forward over the railing, her legs lifting high off the ground. The sensation made her dizzy, as if her stomach were plunging straight out of the soles of her feet.

Inside, Harold called out, "What is Alsace and Lorraine?" Josie's mother got up, nudged the door open, and slipped inside.

Josie kept her back to them. There was a stiff breeze coming from the west, so she folded her legs together and hugged them to her chest. In Social Studies, she'd learned about Alsace and Lorraine, too. Those little provinces in France. But now Harold had quieted down, and Josie could picture them sitting arm-in-arm on the fold-out sofa. She knew they never got any privacy. This was a one-bedroom apartment, and her mom and Harold slept on the couch. Josie slept in the bedroom. When it was just the two of them, before Harold moved in, her mom used to knock softly on the door. She would push the door open, her face creased and pale, her dark hair swinging loose. Josie would pull aside the covers and her mom would clamber in beside her. Even though Josie was fully grown, seventeen years old, she liked sleeping beside her mom. She liked her mom's clean, antiseptic smell. Even though Josie had gotten used to Harold, and she called him "old man," and they yukked it up in front of the same TV programs, she missed the way things were before.

She'd stopped counting the times she'd lain in bed, listening through the walls while her mom had sex with him. Josie even put a pillow over her head to drown it out. She reprimanded herself for listening, called herself a freak, and a loser. Once, she even burst into tears. She flirted with the idea of running into the living room, yelling, "Cut it out!" and then slamming her bedroom door behind her. It infuriated her because she was supposed to be the one with boyfriends, the one illicitly sneaking them home. Josie had a boyfriend, but she suspected that her mom cared more about Harold than Josie cared about Bradley. It was her mom who was the girlish one, the one who daydreamed and doodled and preened in the bathroom. And Josie just sulked on the couch, flipping channels, boring herself to death with television.

She propped her legs up on the balcony railing. Still, she loved Bradley enough. She planned to run away with him. He had asked her, last week. He wanted to be an actor. There was work, he told her, in Toronto. She saw him in a new light then, as someone whose dreams could make her happy. In this apartment, Josie thought she might drown. Her mom tried so hard but it wasn't the same. Now that Harold was here, it would never be the same again.

When Josie was young, she wanted to be a diver. She loved their stretched limbs and taut bodies, their arms cutting the water. Part of her wanted to just dive off this balcony, her body in perfect position while the highrise fell away behind her. Through the backdrop of this city, on and on and on, not caring at all if the water ever came.

The worst thing her mother ever did to Josie was hold her under burning water. She didn't argue that she deserved it. In hindsight, Josie thought she was lucky her mom hadn't lost her temper and smacked her good. The thing was, Josie had only been trying to help.

She had taken the silver-plated bracelet, the one her father, the helicopter pilot, had given her mother, and tied it to the balcony. Her plan was simple. She was sending a message, the same way people used telegraphs, carrier pigeons, or prayer flags. When her father searched the mountains, he might see the chain fluttering from the post. It might catch his eye like a dry spark. At dinner time, she and her mother would see his helicopter hovering outside the patio window, his eyes searching through the glass for them.

She looped a long piece of thread though one end and knotted the thread to a post on the balcony. The bracelet lay flat, but when a gust of wind came, it shook very gently.

Josie left it there while she went to school. She was in grade four. All day she thought of it, a glinting that would stop him, out of the corner of his eye, make him stop in his tracks and look up. When she came home in the afternoon, the piece of thread had come loose from the balcony. The bracelet was gone.

That night, when her mom realized the bracelet was missing, she walked in on Josie in the bath. She held the empty box out. "Sweetheart," she said, "where is Mommy's bracelet?"

Josie dipped her hands into the bathwater. She lowered her eyes. "I lost it."

"Where?"

Josie looked up at her mother. She gave her most innocent smile. "I dropped it," she said, shrugging. "Off the balcony."

Her mom wrenched the hot-water tap on, shower spurting, steam filling the room. The water was burning. Her mom started crying. "You terrible girl!" she said. "You had no right. It was the only thing I ever had." The water burned her skin, it scalded her right to the bone. Josie screamed hysterically. Her mom wrenched the other tap and the water turned freezing cold. Then she pulled Josie out. Josie's skin was raw. "I'm sorry," her mom whispered, all her rage gone. She repeated it over and over again. "I'm sorry, I'm sorry." Josie wished she could go back, retrace her steps, have the bracelet in her hands again before all this happened. For the first time, she looked at her mother in a new light, full of love and hate and incomprehension. Her mom applied an ointment to Josie's skin and kissed the air so her lips wouldn't hurt her.

They slept beside one another that night, and no matter how Josie moved, her mom kept her arms tight around her, and Josie couldn't pry herself loose.

Josie admitted to herself that she didn't really love Bradley. She liked him well enough. She liked the way they held hands and walked through the empty schoolyard. It made her chest burn with warmth, as if from exertion. He called her by her full name, Josephine. She thought it made her seem more important than she really was.

When Josie was a little girl, she had worried that her mother would abandon her. A common fear, she later learned. A sign of the child's first awareness of the encroaching world. She remembered lying on the couch, asking her mother, "Will you always take care of me?" and her mother nodding fervently, "Yes, I always will."

Now, Harold had made her mother's eyes young again. It convinced Josie of what she knew deep down, that she wasn't meant to be here any longer. She recognized a hardness in herself, razor sharp, wanting to be set loose. It wasn't Toronto so much as the fact that she needed to be gone. Whether she went with this boy or on her own, it didn't matter so long as she left here. Last night, she'd struggled with a note to her mom. She'd tried saying it in different ways, but no matter what she wrote she ended up sounding trite.

Before she left, Josie went into the cabinets and took out the plastic bottle of Aspirin. Under the cotton wadding was a roll of bills, her mom's emergency money, in case of earthquakes or disasters. Josie pocketed it, knowing her mother meant it for her. What did they call it back then? Pin money. The words made Josie smile.

She was leaving them something in return — the bedroom, the living room, the kitchen, and the balcony. Years to themselves. A missing child. She loved her mother to death, but that wasn't the kind of thing she could write in a note. They wouldn't believe her anyway. They would never understand how much thought Josie had put into this, how much she missed them already. On a scrap of paper, she wrote that she would call soon.

When Harold walked into the kitchen and saw the money in her hands and the rucksack on the floor, he guessed everything. He said, "If you do this, you're going to break your mother's heart."

"She'll recover." She and Harold stood facing each other, like cowboys in a Western, hands loose at their sides. Josie didn't know whether to fight or run. Replacing the cap on the plastic bottle, she said, "I tried to tell her. You heard me trying."

Harold stared down at the linoleum floor, down at his worn slippers. "I heard you." When he said this, he gazed at her steadily and Josie had a glimpse of Harold as a young boy. Stubborn, relentless in his own patient way. He surprised her. "Better leave now, before she gets home."

She was running late. She swung her rucksack up. The weight pulled her back and she had to grasp the walls for support. Harold opened the door for her, and Josie turned to him quickly, planting a kiss on his cheek. Then she took the elevator down seventeen floors, and walked calmly through the glass entrance. She started to run. She was holding her coat in her right hand. The grass was wet and her coat dragged along the grass. Josie imagined that the sound of her coat in the grass was her mother running behind her. She was pulling at Josie's arms and legs, and begging her not to go. And Josie didn't know what to tell her, so they just kept running like that, across parking lots and front lawns. She was sweating, and the rucksack bounced painfully against her shoulders. Her friend, the boy with the dark hair and brown eyes, was holding the passenger door open for her. Sliding in, Josie pictured herself falling out of the sky, the bag in her arms, highrise blurred in the backdrop.

¤

In the end, Josie will not marry the boy with the dark hair and the brown eyes. She will move on from him and from a dozen other men and women. A decade later, when Thea's hair is fully white and Harold has put on too much weight, she will go home once more and sleep in her old bedroom. But it won't be for long. Soon she'll be on the move again because something in her can't rest, something inside her fights it tooth and nail. Over the years, Josie will ask herself, *What are you running away from?* Each time, she will answer the question differently. *Because I can* is the answer she likes best. Josie will tell people that she has always been a free spirit. Some men will think she is asking them, obliquely, to pin her down, to give her a reason to stay. They will ask her, "Don't you want a family?" and she'll laugh at them, say, "I already have one." She leaves these ones faster than the rest.

When standing on high landings — balconies, suspension bridges, look-outs — she still has the compulsion to jump. She believes in her own recklessness. It is the only faith she has.

When she is very old and she has set foot in most of the countries in the world, Josie will tell her friends that her father was a boy who jumped from a roof and her mother was a woman who fell from a helicopter. They will know she is lying but she will never tell them *how*, or which details of the story are true. Until she dies, she will wonder about her real father and the twists and turns that have marked his life. She tries to imagine his helicopter, the people he has saved, or more importantly, the ones he has lost. All her life, Josie will wonder how she bypassed love when it was the very reason for, the root, of her disappearance. When people ask, she will say that her favorite country is one that has not yet been discovered.

A Map of the City

In the years after I left home, I used to glimpse my parents in unexpected places. I would see the two of them in the Safeway, my mother standing patiently by while my father weighed oranges in his hands, feeling for signs of imperfection. I would see them on the opposite sidewalk, blurred and old, traffic streaming between us. During these sightings, I never felt the urge to join them. I only wanted to remain where I was and watch while they negotiated their way through the aisles, their bodies slow with old age.

Of course, it was never them. By this time, my father had returned from Indonesia and my mother was living alone in an apartment outside of the city. I had not seen my parents side by side in almost a decade. It would be some other couple, vague and kindly looking, who would catch my eye, remind me of things I thought I had long forgotten.

My husband Will once said that longing manifests itself in sight. In therapy groups, people tell of seeing their loved ones long after they have passed away — a father, sitting in his usual armchair, a sister in the garden.

To Will, I said that longing was not the point. In any case, my parents were still alive.

Will said, "Death isn't what I meant exactly. And don't be so sure about the longing."

"Why not?"

"Because it's plain. You miss them all the time."

I let this sit for a moment, then I broke into a smile. Will was unfailingly patient. He let me dance around a topic but never come to rest on it. He forgave all my inabilities, first and foremost my unwillingness to speak with him about my family.

At first, this allowed me to put all my energy into the here and now, our present life. In hindsight, I see it also freed me to walk away, at least for a period of time, from certain obligations. I asked myself, does my family have any hold on me? For a long time, I tried to say *no*. We would remain separate from each other until the end. But then Will and I married, and when I thought about my own future, the possibility of children, I saw how the tables had turned. *Yes*, I realized. Their hold would never diminish. For the first time I was struck by the disarray of my life. Walking away had not saved me as I had hoped it would.

My father used to own a furniture store.

That is a sentence I might have said to Will, but I can't recall now exactly which details I gave him.

My father used to own a furniture store and the store was named Bargain Mart. The front was made entirely of glass. A big white awning sheltered the entrance. I still remember that, when I was a child, my grade-one teacher singled me out. "Oh, yes," she said. "It's your father who owns that store, isn't it? The furniture store on Hastings Street."

I nodded proudly. Even to me, at that age, the idea of ownership meant something. Along Hastings Street was the bakery, the deli, the children's clothing store, the light shop. My father's furniture store was one among these and it had its place in the accepted order of things.

On weekends, I assisted my father. I turned over the *Closed* sign. Together, we sprayed Windex on the front windows. The couches were used, or sold on consignment, so you could find an armchair for ten or fifteen dollars, a sofa for thirty. When my father made a sale, he let me deliver the receipt and change to the customer, which I did proudly.

I was six years old then, and I dreamed commercials. In my mind, my father was the owner of an exciting retail outlet. Soon the furniture store would be a household word: *Bargain Mart.* Parents would announce to their children that this weekend's excursion would be to *Bargain Mart,* and children across the city would look up from their Cream of Wheat and cheer. From where we lived in Burnaby, in the spill of houses beneath the mountain, to Maple Ridge and Vancouver, people would flock to my father's store, carting away sofas on their shoulders, tables in their arms. My father standing at the front, hands on his hips, young.

My parents were thirty when they emigrated from Indonesia. The first business they owned in Vancouver was a restaurant, the All Day Grill. My father cooked up steak and eggs, sweet and sour pork on rice, and beef dip sandwiches.

I was born shortly after they arrived in Canada. When I was five months old, the doctors diagnosed me with kidney failure. This is what my mother told me — after twelve hours of cooking at the restaurant, my father would drive to the hospital. He would sweep into the nursery and gather me in his arms, careful of all my intravenous tubes. We paced the hallway, my father rolling the IV pole ahead of us. My mother says I recognized him. In his arms, I was peaceful, but when he returned me to my bed, I wailed and fought. The nurses complained that each time my father left, I threw tantrums then shredded my cotton blanket with my tiny hands. I lost a kidney, but came out of the hospital when I was one. The restaurant went under.

Perhaps because of this, my father would often say that I had ruined his life. This was never said in a malicious manner, or one meant to wound me. It was matter-of-fact, the way one might speak of a change in the weather or an accident far away. If something was troubling him, my father would give a slow shake of his head. "Ever since you were born, Miriam, my life has been terrible." The smallest hint of a smile.

When I tell people this, laughing, they shake their heads in disbelief. I suppose I can understand how these words might sound to a stranger. Insensitive. Cruel. But this is not so. Between my father and me there was always a tacit understanding. Despite the teasing, he had an unwavering faith in me. "My daughter, Miriam," he said to everyone. "When she grows up, she is going to buy her parents a big house."

I would hold on to his hand when he said this, my face glowing with pride.

Of course my father never expected such things from me. It was only a joke, a laughing aside to tell me that his faith in me was abundant. Still, in the years after I left home, I wanted it to be true. I wanted to present my father with a house, hand him the key to his perfect life. By that time, he was living alone. The years had taken their toll on my family and he was estranged from my mother and me.

I needed to ask him, *Have I disappointed you?* but the question itself seemed too simple. What kind of answer could he give? We had failed each other in so many unintended ways and then we had drifted apart. My father seemed lost in the past and I did not trust myself to guide him into the present. So I kept my distance and thought from time to time how things might have turned out differently. If I had been the kind of daughter I never was, faithful and capable, who could hold a family together through all its small tragedies.

Bargain Mart, with its hall of couches, is now a restaurant. The floor-to-ceiling glass nicely curtained. Ethiopian, my mother thinks, or is it Japanese? Some mornings I wake up remembering the store, not how it looked inside but how it looked when you stood at the front, at the glass, the view of the street and the stores across. It is not the kind of place you can find so easily now, a neighborhood furniture store, family-owned.

As a child, I faked illness in order to be taken there. Once, I tiptoed into the bathroom and held the

blow-dryer up to my face. Then I stood at my parents'
bedside. Two hands pressed to my stomach, I whispered, "Ache." A pause. Then, "*Ache.*" My mother eyed
me suspiciously. But my father, somehow, believed me.
He held the palm of his hand to my forehead and his
face filled with worry.

While I lounged in bed, my father brought me
Eggo waffles, a glass of milk, and one tablet of Aspirin
crushed soft as sand. Then he called my grade-one
teacher to tell her I was sick again. Instead of school,
he would take me with him to the furniture store.

Together, we walked across the front lawn, the
cold grass crunching like snow under our shoes. I held
both hands over my stomach and watched my breath
unroll ahead of me, a white windsock. My father
scraped ice off the windshield in scratchy lines, he
leaned his body far across the car, arms out like a
swimmer. After he was done, we sat in silence, watching the ice melt in little triangles off the windshield.
When the car was warm enough, my father said,
"Okay," and I replied, "Okay." We rolled forward on
the grass. He turned down the alley, exhaust lifting
like a plume behind us. The car lumbered down
Hastings Street, past the bakery and the deli and the
light shop.

In front of the store, we stood shivering on the
sidewalk while my father fit the key into the lock.

When the door jingled open, the lemony smell of cleanser wafted out. My father mopped the floors every night before closing and the scent stayed trapped inside until morning. In the store, all the couches seemed to call to me — the creaky recliner, the velvet loveseat. I ran ahead of him into the maze of sofas.

Along one wall there was a closet storage room. It had no door and my father had hung a shower curtain there instead. On my sick days, I slept inside the closet. My bed was a plastic lawn chair. When customers began to arrive, my father pulled the shower curtain closed so that I could sleep.

"Dad," I said once, unable to see around the corner to where he was sitting. "What are you doing right now?"

"Right now? I'm trying to imagine what other people see when they come into the store."

"How come?"

He paused thoughtfully. "I'm the salesman. I must understand the buying patterns. Then I can find some way to convince them that they need this couch or that chair."

"Oh," I said. "It's like an argument."

"A bit like one. Only there's no fighting. Just persuasion. That's the beauty of my job. The best salesmen do that, they convince you to see their point of view."

There was a radio he kept on his desk at the

back, and he sang along to John Denver, "Take Me Home, Country Roads," his voice filled with gusto. "You look a little like him," my father joked. "With those ears on you."

I climbed out of the lawn chair. Walking in my bare feet, I took my father by the hand, pointing out the pieces I liked. "Don't sell this one while I'm at school," I told him. "Or this one. I put my name on it." He looked at the scrawl in blue crayon on the upholstery: *Miriam.* No anger. Too tired, maybe, like the time I begged him to let me mow the lawn and I promptly ran over the electrical cord, severing it in two. No anger there, either.

In the closet, I could always get a feel for the way things were going in the store. Rarely was business brisk. My father was not the type to push anyone into a purchase. "Big commitment to buy a couch," he said to one person. "It's important to be sure."

To someone else, he said, "This piece here? Oh, yes. See the way it reclines. Very smoothly. Just like new. Yes, a very good price."

On the other side of the shower curtain, a pair of shoes stopped and waited. A low whistle. The man talked about inflation, the way a dollar just didn't go as far as it used to.

"Yes," my father replied, his voice filled with sympathy. "That is very true."

The shower curtain opened suddenly and I was blinded by light. "Jesus Christ," the man said, stepping backwards, his hand dropping the curtain.

My father hurried forward. "My daughter, she is resting."

The man stared at me, aghast. I smiled helpfully.

"No problem, no problem." My father nodded at me and yanked the shower curtain closed.

"I'm very sorry. I didn't realize," his voice trailed off.

"No problem," my father said again, boisterously. "She is resting only."

Their feet disappeared from sight, the door jingling soon after.

That afternoon, I watched my father read the newspaper, cover to cover, retaining names and news for his casual conversation. "Trudeau," he said to one customer, then shrugged his shoulders, or "Bill Bennett," or "Thatcherism," the word hanging disturbingly in the air.

Outside, rain poured down in thin streams off the white awning, splashing the sidewalk. There was a lull and my father reached into his desk and pulled out a handful of photographs. I had seen them before, Indonesian plantations spread out under wide skies. He tapped his index finger down, pointing out the house where my parents lived before coming to Vancouver. Stilts like legs holding it off the ground. My father ran his hands over the trees in the backdrop, told me about the fruit, strange and exotic things, rambutan and durians. From memory, he sketched a map of Irian Jaya — the shape like a half-torso, one arm waving — where my parents had lived for a short time. "Do you miss it?" I asked him.

"What's to miss?" he said, smiling gently.

I didn't know.

"I only miss the fruit," he said, putting the photos away. "The country, I've almost forgotten."

My father and I played tic-tac-toe until six o'clock, and then my father closed the store. While he counted the cash, I washed the floor, dragging the mop behind me as I paced back and forth. Eventually, my father took the mop from me and scrubbed diligently at the scuff marks and water stains. Then he turned the lights down and locked the door behind us. We drove home in the Buick, past the Knight and Day Restaurant that had burned down three times in the last two years. My father pointed through the windshield. "See that restaurant?" he said. "That restaurant's burning down *night and day*." He laughed almost hysterically.

At home, my father washed the vegetables for dinner. I set the table so that everything was ready by the time my mother came home at seven, exhausted from her job at the tire store.

Over dinner, my parents inquired after each other's day. My mother spooned some liver onto my plate, wondering aloud why I might be sick. "Did you eat something bad?" she asked.

"Here," my father said, lifting his chopsticks towards me. "Eat more vegetables."

Afterwards, as he was clearing the dishes, they worried over the day's receipts. Only two small sales. "January is like this," my father said. "It's to be expected."

"December was like this too," my mother replied.

"It will pick up."

My mother sighed. "It will have to."

She and I lay down on the couch to watch television. She fell asleep almost instantly, her face buried in my neck.

That night, I slept between them. They stayed on far sides of the bed, me in the middle drifting from one side to another in all their empty space. In the morning, my mother woke first. I could see her in the dark, reaching for her clothes. When I waved goodbye, she hovered above me, planting a kiss on my forehead. Then she kissed my father. By the time he opened his eyes, she was already dressed and gone.

¤

I have lived in Vancouver all my life. I seldom pass through the old alleys and neighborhoods where I grew up, but when I do my memory astonishes me. How can it be that this street is exactly the way I remember it? I look for the passage of twenty years, find it only in the height of the trees. But the street itself is the same, the crosswalk and stop sign, the broken pavement, *step on a crack, break your mother's back,* the glass storefronts.

When I was twenty-one, the familiarity of this city comforted me. I was waitressing then, working odd jobs. Every night my girlfriends and I stayed late at the bar, lighting cigarettes, throwing shots of vodka straight back. Men came and went; it was nothing. Some nights, we dropped our clothes on the sand and swam in the ocean. Bitterly cold, it shocked us sober. Other times, I drove along the coast, the sky blacked out. I'd park and watch the big green trees rolling back and forth in the wind and the sight would make me fleetingly happy. Legs stretched out, I would lie back on the roof of my car and listen to the sound of my clothes flapping.

It was around this time that I met Will. He lived in an apartment down the alley from me, and I used to sit on my back porch watching him come and go. I liked his gray eyes, which seemed dignified on such a boyish face. He had a tall, stooped body and thin, wavy hair. Will has a straightforward sort of face, an open book. It's the face of an innocent, no secrets in it. Everything laid out, plain and simple.

One day I saw him coming down the alley on his motorcycle, a beautifully beat-up old thing. I walked out into his path and stood in front of him. I said I'd seen him coming and going, heard his motorcycle late at night when I couldn't sleep.

He looked at me, confused and a little embarrassed.

"I just have this feeling," I said, swaying back and forth on my feet, "that we are meant to be."

He looked at me searchingly. A surprised smile. "Who am I to argue?" he said, when he finally spoke. That was good enough for me.

That night, he brought me a helmet and fastened the straps under my chin. "Through this hoop and then back again, just like a backpack. Put your feet there," he nodded at two pedals, "and watch the pipe, it could melt your boots. It gets pretty hot. You'll find that sometimes I'll put the brakes on and our heads will collide. Don't worry, it doesn't throw me off. You can hold on here. Lean right back."

We lunged forward. I held on to his waist. The wind knocked every thought from my head. On every straight piece of road, he hit the accelerator and we seemed to lift.

At a stop light, he turned around, flipping up his visor. "I can't breathe."

"No," I said. "Me neither."

"I can't breathe when you squeeze my stomach. Can

you hold me here?" He lifted my arms to his chest.

Oncoming cars drilled past us. We leaned into a curve, highway veering up. I held on for dear life. He turned around, mouthing, "Okay?"

"Okay."

The palms of my hands were flat overtop of his heart. I worried I would stop his breathing, give him a heart attack. Sometimes I could see his face in the side mirror. The back of his body, his white shirt flapping in the wind, was touchingly vulnerable. One wrong move and we'd be flying. Me, him, and the bike coming apart in the sky.

When we stopped I was out of breath. "More?" he asked.

I nodded.

"What does it feel like?"

"Like I can't get enough of it."

On the way back to the city, the moon was low and full, a bright orange round above the skyline. The mountains bloomed against sky, one after the other like an abundance of shadows. I remember watching one silent tanker floating on the water. We sped over the Lions Gate Bridge, a chain of lights. I grasped his chest, kept my eyes wide open, and thought, *Things should always come this easy.*

That night I dreamed that I would never wake up. When I did, startled, exhilarated, Will was half on top of me, one bare arm reaching across my stomach, still sleeping.

Some facts seem, at first, to explain a person. Will's mother died of cancer when he was young. His father died not long after, an electrical accident at the plant where he worked. When I first walked into Will's apartment, I thought it was an elegy, a place of grief. But no, Will said he just liked to keep things simple. The walls bare, the furniture nonexistent. Will slept on a mat on the floor. The living room housed his books, stacked in pyramids. He taught art history at one of the nearby colleges.

I admired his restraint. To me, his apartment was the embodiment of his uncluttered life, exactly the kind of life I aspired to — both feet planted, eyes on the future. The present tripped me up. I was forever sorting out my bearings. Will, on the other hand, was tuned towards a distant point. It seemed to me, then, that the troubles of day-to-day life would never burden him as they did ordinary people. Will was also fearless and I loved this in him. He jumped headlong into our relationship, throwing caution to the wind.

The wedding was fast, the kind that's over in half an hour and then you're outside, pictures flashing, thinking, *What just happened?* but overcome by happiness the whole time. During the ceremony we couldn't stop laughing. Even saying our vows. Will's face was lit up like a kid's and I started laughing so hard I had to bend over, holding my stomach. A bit of hair was sticking up at the side of his head and I reached out to smooth it down. We were all laughing inside the church and even my mom, hair full of gray now, couldn't find a moment to cry.

We had rushed into marriage. I always joked it was the motorcycle that did it, swept me off my feet, and he would say, "I know it." I had no words to describe how exhausted I was that night when I walked into the alley in front of him. Afraid of everything. I thought I'd give it one last go, talk to him. At that time, something in my life was eating away at me. I couldn't shake it. And there was Will, always on the move. I should just grab hold.

¤

My father was not present at our wedding. He called in the early morning, his voice weak and sorry. "A cold," he said, "has knocked me down."

It did not surprise me, my father's last-minute decision. At that time, he was living alone. When he left my mother, some years earlier, he had stepped away into a different kind of life, one where family obligations no longer weighed so heavily. In some ways, by leaving, he gave my mother and me our freedom. We moved on with our lives while he remained in the background, the one we had never understood. Who took his own failures so much to heart, he could no longer see past them, and obliged them by leaving.

My father rarely tried to contact me. I believed, then, that he had chosen his own circumstances and imposed solitude on himself. In some ways, this came as a relief to me. When Will and I married, I was twenty-one years old and I didn't want to take my eyes off the future.

Years ago, it was a different story. My parents and I would drive across the city, going nowhere in partic-ular, all of us bundled into the Buick. Through down-town and Chinatown — those narrow streets flooded with people — then out to the suburbs. On the highway, we caught glimpses of ocean, blue and sudden.

I was the only one of us born in Canada, and so I prided myself on knowing Vancouver better than my parents did — the streets, Rupert, Renfrew, Nanaimo, Victoria. Ticking them off as we passed each set of lights, *go, go, go. Stop.*

But nothing in Vancouver had the ring of Irian Jaya, where my parents lived in the first years of their marriage. In 1963, the country was annexed by Indonesia. They outlawed the Papuan flag, named the territory Irian Jaya, and flooded their own people onto the island. My parents, Chinese-Indonesians, arrived during this wave and lived there through the 1960s. "There were no roads," my father said, on one of our long Sunday drives. "Nothing."

My mother nodded her head. "The aborigines came into Jayapura looking for work. It was a rough town. Like a frontier. And the fighting. Do you remember the stories?" She shivered, one hand floating down to rest on my father's knee.

"People thrown from helicopters. The Indonesian army threw resistance fighters into their own valleys. There were many rumors."

Despite the violence and the political tension, my parents missed Indonesia. It came out in small ways, their English interrupted by a word of Chinese, a word of Indonesian. The exotic exclamations at the end of their sentences, *ah yah!*, or calling me to dinner, *makan, makan.* My mother told me that *irian*, a Biak word, means "place of the volcano" and that *jaya*, an Indonesian word, means "success." But those were the only Indonesian words I learned. At home, they spoke Indonesian and Chinese only to each other, never to me. My mother would stand on the porch watching kids race their bikes up and down the back lane, and say, out of the blue, "But isn't it so much cleaner here?"

In 1969, the United Nations led a vote, the "Act of Free Choice," to allow the Irianese to determine their future. The Irianese voted to become part of Indonesia. "Rigged," my mother told me, her eyes clouding. "And everyone knew it."

My parents said the resistance attacked the gold and copper mines. The Indonesian army, unable to penetrate the jungle, swept through villages. They burned them to the ground and people disappeared. My parents decided it was time to leave. They gave up their Indonesian citizenship for good.

"In Irian Jaya," my father told me, "the road stops dead at the jungle. If you want to reach the next town, you must go by boat or plane. You can't just get in your car and drive there." My father was suspicious of Canadian highways, the very ease of crossing such a country.

Perhaps he drove to test them. On those Sunday drives, we piled into the car, my father losing us in side streets, winding us along highways. In winter, the roads were icy with rain but we hurtled through the dark roads anyway, gutters of water shooting sky-high.

On Sundays, the furniture store was closed. Month after month, the old sofas and chairs remained unsold, and my parents fell further behind on their mortgage payments. All the savings they had brought with them from Indonesia seemed to trickle in a thin river out the door, down the street, to some place from which we would never recover it. My family's luck, if a family could have luck, was running dry.

This was the high point, the three of us packed in the car, my mother's voice wavering thin and high over the words on the radio. We didn't know how peaceful we were. Only years later, when my father lay in the Intensive Care Unit at Vancouver General Hospital, a thick tube in his throat to carry his breathing, did it strike me just how much we had changed and how far away that earlier time had gone.

¤

There is my mother, the navigator, a map of the city unfurled on her lap. Me in the back seat, watching my father's eyes as they glance in the rear-view mirror, the way he searches for what might appear. Now, with the distance of time, I look back at my parents differently — I try to re-read their gestures, the trajectory of these events. If I change the way shadow and light play on them, will I find one more detail? Some small piece that I could not see before.

In the first years of my own marriage, I could not look beyond Will. Our day-to-day routine was calming to me. He brought a certain contentment to my life, a settled happiness that I had not yet experienced.

When he read late at night, I fell asleep to the scratching of his pencil, the sound of a page turning. Sometimes he would nudge me awake, show me a photograph. The spires of the Angkor Wat, or a rock painting unearthed on the Tulare River. Will has an open heart, he can see the mystery in anything. When he tapped a photo with his index finger, I allowed myself to move with him, swept up in one idea and then another, losing myself in Will's generous imagination. I opened myself up to it, letting this old history settle over my own small past.

¤

By the time I was seven, the furniture store had fallen on hard times. I still accompanied my father after school or on weekends. More and more, I caught him resting. He would be sitting on a couch, looking out the window, just waiting. He had always been a restrained man, and whatever emotions he carried, he kept well hidden. Looking around at the couches and the chairs, my father simply waited in silence, turning his head at the sound of the door opening.

One night at dinner, my mother bowed her head. "We better sell now," she said, her voice low.

Beside me, my father ate quietly, bowl held in one hand, his chopsticks lifting slowly.

"There is nothing else we can do. We can't afford it any more."

I pretended I wasn't listening, the polite thing to do. I kept eating, with my legs swinging quietly under the table.

"What about the mortgage?" she asked, shaking her head. "We can't pay the mortgage or the car payments. At this rate we will lose the house, not just the store. Please, don't be so stubborn."

My father pushed his plate away, then stood up and left the table. Beside me, my mother sighed and continued eating. When she was done, she pushed her chair back and went upstairs. I was always the last one. Sitting on my own, I'd forget all about dinner and let my mind wander. Sometimes I was still there at nine or ten at night, lost in thought, my bowl still half full. All the light in the kitchen gone so I would curl my legs up on the chair and rest my face on the table. Small bits of rice stuck to my cheek. Eventually my mother would come and take the bowl away.

That night, my parents went into the bedroom to argue. Their voices were faint through the house like a distant television. Someone slammed a door hard. Eventually I got up and tipped my own bowl of food over the garbage. When I went upstairs to bed, all the doors were closed and the house was quiet.

The next morning, my parents started up again. I was already sitting at the table, eating breakfast.

My father came out of the bedroom and circled the kitchen table. "What do you want me to do? What do I do when the store is sold?"

"Go back to school. Do something for yourself, make yourself employable."

"I am employed. I'm working as hard as I can. Is it so disappointing to you, everything that I have done?"

She shook her head impatiently. "Don't be ridiculous."

I stared from one to the other. My father laughed suddenly. It was a harsh sound, sad and bitter. He smiled, one hand waving up into the air then falling slowly. "Who is it?" he asked.

"What do you mean?"

"The one at work, the one who promoted you."

"I don't know what you're talking about."

"What did he do that for, promote you? In Indonesia you couldn't hold down a job. Here, a promotion. I can't understand it."

My mother looked at him in disbelief. "I was miserable there. You know that."

"You tell me," he said, his voice even. "How is this possible? Remember, you are the one who wanted to leave Irian Jaya. It is because of you that we are in this situation."

My mother burst into tears. "This has nothing to do with who you are and who I am. I am only trying to do what is best for us."

I stood then, picking up my plate. My hands were shaking and the dish tipped, spilling milk and cereal. My father looked at me, then turned towards the sink. He picked up a cloth and ran it, end to end, across the table. Then he turned back to my mother. "I do not think so," he said. "And it is not your decision."

My mother picked up her purse and walked out the back door, the screen swinging behind her.

"I'm doing the best I can," my father said. "Your mother, she wants everything. Do you see that? She wants everything."

I tried hard to behave as I'd been brought up, to ignore what I was not involved in and to hold my tongue and pretend I was deaf and blind. Eyes lowered, I stared at the table.

Afterwards, when he bundled me up and walked me to school, he said nothing. He let go of me and I ran into the schoolyard, immersed myself in hop-scotch and California kickball. I would adapt. He knew I would grow up and do well here. My father turned around, he started walking home again.

For six more months, the store pushed on. Whenever my father thought he might have to give in, somebody came along and bought a couch. A sofa here, a loveseat there — this somehow kept us going from week to week.

Now, looking back, I see that the store had an impoverished look to it, that the couches were old and worn, and that my father, once so patient a sales-man, had begun to speak to his customers with an air of quiet desperation. At home, my parents had fallen into a deep silence, speaking to each other only when necessary. "Tell your mother that . . . ," my father said, and I was thrown out like a line between them.

On the weekends, I kept my father company in the store. Sometimes, during the afternoon lulls, I fell asleep on the lawn chair. Once, just waking, I sat up and listened for my father's movements, the creak of his chair, his shoes on the polished floor. There were no sounds at all. Thinking he had disappeared, I pulled the curtain open and ran out. I can see myself, a small girl in blue sweatpants and a faded T-shirt, my John Denver ears, all keyed up. He was sitting at his desk. I looked at his face, his furrowed brow, and asked, "Is there something wrong?"

He looked at me for a long time, his expression melancholy. Then he said, "No. There is nothing to worry about."

Not long after, the bank sent my father a letter saying they were foreclosing on our mortgage. When we moved out of our house on Curtis Street, my father would be the one who packed. While my mother kept me occupied on the back lawn, he would go from room to room, throwing everything into bags, my mother's good dresses and shoes, my toys and socks. Driving away to our new apartment, we would turn back to the house, catch a glimpse of our excess furniture lined up on the sidewalk, the line of boxes and Glad bags stretching down the block.

But that day in the furniture store, my father was calm. He stood up from his desk and walked to the door. He turned the sign over and said to me, "I don't think anyone else is coming today." My father gathered my crayons and drawings and I started telling him about the book I was reading, Dumbo and the crows and how at the end he flies and his mother who cradles him in her trunk. My father just looked at me. This was the last business he would ever own.

That was the end of it. I don't recall stepping inside the store again. When I saw it next, the windows were papered over so that I could no longer see the interior from the road.

¤

The other day, my father telephoned to give me the news. "Fighting in Aceh," he says. "And another ferry has gone down."

I tell him about Will's new teaching position.

He says, "That's very good news."

This new relationship we have is tentative, like moving in the dark. A step forward, then back, feeling for the perimeter of the room.

"Are you free?" I ask. "We can have coffee."

"I can't drink coffee," he says. "It gives me heart-burn."

I file this information away, then I suggest tea.

Silence, as he considers this. "Will you come in the car? I'm having some problems with my knees."

"Of course."

When I hang up the phone, I feel a surge of hope, of fierce protectiveness over him. Perhaps, knowing everything that has brought us here, I would redraw this map, make the distance from A to B a straight line. I would bypass those difficult years and bring my father up to this moment, healthy, unharmed.

But to do so would remove all we glimpsed in passing, heights and depths I never guessed at. That straight line would erase our efforts, the necessary ones as well as the misguided ones, that finally allowed us to arrive here.

¤

In the summers, Will and I left Vancouver at every opportunity. When the college shut down after spring semester, we headed out along the west coast. I was doing secretarial jobs then, temp work in law firms or ad agencies. I loved the transience of it, learning a routine then forgetting it in place of another.

Once, we spent the week in Neah Bay. I had set my finger down on the map, touched the western-most reach of the Olympic Peninsula. "Here," I said, turning to Will. "I'd like to go here." We raced the motorcycle south, then west. The town sat high on a cliff of rocks overlooking the Pacific Ocean. That first night, in our tiny motel room, Will told me that piercing a lime with pins is said to cause pain for the person you love. "That's it," I said. "We're throwing all the limes out."

He smiled. "Who needs limes?"

"Not us."

"But children, on the other hand."

"To cause us pain?" I said, laughing.

When he didn't respond, I looked over at him. Will's face was serious. He pushed himself up on one arm. "It scares me too. But let's think about it. It won't be so terrible. We can get a car seat for the motorcycle. We can get a baby helmet. Our lives won't change so much."

"Okay, I'll think about it."

He rolled over on top of me. Some emotion, fleeting and sad, hit me then. "What's wrong?" he asked, moving his fingers against my face. "I haven't been near any limes."

I smiled, circling my arms around his neck. We could do this, I thought, if I didn't stop to think. We could have the kind of future Will imagined and that I, in moments of abandon, admitted that I wanted too. Outside I could hear cars on the gravel road, here and gone, the shifting pebbles. Will picked my hand up and I should have said then what I feared. Instead, I allowed the moment to pass. I let it drop there like glass in the sand.

¤

After the furniture store closed so many years before, my parents declared bankruptcy. In the years that followed, they lived from hand to mouth. My mother took on a second job in order to support us. My father tried his hand at different careers. For a time, he cooked in an Indonesian restaurant. Afterwards, he sold encyclopedias, door to door; then cars at the Ford dealership. Finally, my father went into real estate. I was fourteen years old and I would follow him to Open Houses. Sunday mornings, the city half asleep, we loaded my father's signs into the trunk of his car: *Open House Today*, they said, *Come on in!* He planted them in the soft ground, into the dewy grass.

For years, my father sold "Vancouver Specials." Two bedrooms up, one down, they spanned the east side. Cut-out houses, prefab. In his gray polyester suit, my father never did what other agents did. He never brought flowers to set in the foyer, he never sprayed air fresheners or adjusted the lighting. He just tapped his fingers on the steering wheel, shaking his head at the outside lawn.

When visitors came, he bustled out, all smiles and handshakes, ushering them up the stairs. I sat on the grass reading. I could hear them from the

balcony, their offhand negotiations. The wife, sur-
veying the neighborhood: "Yes, but it's not quite
what I had in mind."

"No? Oh, well, how about —"

"Three-fifty you say? For this side of town?"

For years, my father wore the same suit, loaded the
same signs into the trunk of the same car, and drove
away. At first, he was optimistic. If he was on the verge
of a sale, he paced nervously around the apartment.
"We'll buy a new television," he promised my mother.
"We'll finally take a vacation." My mother would smile,
hopeful. But time and again, his sales fell through.
Perhaps he was too polite, too restrained. He could
never close the deal, to use his words. My father pored
over real estate listings, read articles and books, attended
seminars. He labored over the wording of his pitches.
But if there was a housing boom, it bypassed him. My
father looked on, uncomprehending, while the tide of
wealth and prosperity passed before his very eyes.

One afternoon, he quit. He came home from an
Open House, laid his signs and business cards, his
book of listings beside the garbage. To my mother
and me, seated on the couch, he said, "I'm through."
He left her sitting there, wordless.

In their difficult times, at the first mention of money,
my father would shut down, close his eyes and ears.

He told my mother, over and over, that it had always been her decision to leave Indonesia, and never his. She had separated him from the country he loved. My father once told me that when he came to Canada, his luck had run out. Everything he touched turned bitter. He looked around at our apartment, the old, sagging couches and plastic runners, and blamed himself. He believed his lack of luck, of ingenuity, had done this to us, forced us to struggle for what he failed to provide.

Our apartment became a silent place. My parents chose not to speak, rather than risk an argument that would shatter their fragile peace.

I longed to be free of them. Some nights, I climbed out my window, inched my way to the fire escape. I dropped silently down to the ground. In those still hours between midnight and dawn, I stepped into different cars. Out on the empty highways, my friends and I sped until the trees and the lights ran together. Some nights I let a hand stray across the seats, find its way to the small of my back. A triangle of warmth on my skin.

During these car rides, I thought of my parents fast asleep at home, tossing in dreams. I was glad to be outside, fully awake, racing away from the example of their love. It did not have to be that way, I thought. I could set myself on a different course, walk in the opposite direction.

One night, my mother heard me climb back through my window. She came into my room just as I was getting into bed. "Where have you been?" she asked, exhaustion lining her face. Outside, the car circled the block, around and around, the sound reminding me of wild animals protecting their young, wordless comfort. I didn't answer her, and she rested her warm hands on my forehead. Whatever protection, whatever security they once gave me, was fast disappearing. My mother must have known that, too. She stroked my hair until my breathing slowed. I feigned sleep while she watched over me.

If I walked with my father then, we walked in almost perfect silence. Through the vegetable stands, my father walked ahead of me, his eyebrows creased in thought. He lifted stalks of broccoli, bags of snow peas, weighing them in one hand and then the other. He would ask me, "Which do you prefer?"

And I would shrug, impatient, pushing the grocery cart straight ahead.

"Where's the fire? You're like your mother. Always in a rush. Always needing to be someplace else."

I was fifteen years old and couldn't understand what he wanted from me. I kept on walking.

Each month, I watched my mother sort through the bills, her face blank. She'd open her checkbook, hold the pen in her hand, then stay that way, unsure. My father began swallowing pills, Aspirin or some kind of anti-depressant. His actions became slow and meticulous. He said my mother and I made no sense to him. We rushed everywhere, we didn't have a moment to lose. He, on the other hand, stopped answering the phone. It drove my mother mad. "What if it was important?" she asked him once, after trying all day to reach him.

My father shrugged.

"An emergency? What if Miriam was hurt?"

He looked at her with an expression of complete and utter indifference.

She held her hands up to her ears. "I cannot speak to you. I cannot get through to you. Where have you gone?"

One night, at three in the morning when I was up late, reading, he knocked on the door of my room. "Come in," I said.

He pushed the door open and stood waiting, old and tired. It bothered me to see him there, his disappointment so plainly evident.

"Are you all right, Miriam?" he asked.

"I'm fine."

"I saw your light on. Why are you still awake?"

"I didn't feel like sleeping."

He said, "You shouldn't be staying out so late at night. It's dangerous."

I nodded.

"There's something we need to talk about," my father said.

He stood there waiting for me to answer. I lifted my head up. "I don't want to talk about anything right now."

"Listen." My father's expression, as if on the brink of speech. He looked so soft, standing there. I could touch him and it would hurt. "There's something I need to tell you."

"Not now, please."

"Are you sure?"

I lowered my eyes again. Whatever it was, I didn't want to know. My parents seemed so childlike to me, so in need of love. I thought they only had themselves to blame that I didn't know how to give it to them. For too long, I had been the line between them, the message carrier. Suddenly, I wanted no part in it. I was willing to cut the string and see where we landed. "Yes," I said. "I'm sure."

My father turned around. He went into his bedroom and shut the door behind him.

On a windy, spring day, my father left. He packed a suitcase, bought a plane ticket to Indonesia, and dis-appeared.

That afternoon, when I came home from school, I noticed that my father's bedroom door was ajar. I stood in the hallway listening for him. There was no sound, so I walked inside. The room was neat and clean, the desk bare. For a second, I thought I should turn around and leave. There was something so personal about this abandoned room, so private. But I went to the closet and pulled the doors open. There were two shirts hanging at opposite ends, and nothing else.

I sat down on my father's bed. After a moment, I reached across and opened the desk drawer. There was an envelope with my name on it, as if my father knew, instinctively, that I would do this, look for some clue from him. Inside the envelope was a birthday card. It was early. My sixteenth birthday was still two weeks away. My father wrote that he had returned to Indonesia and that he would call me. There was nothing else.

I opened the curtains, afternoon sunlight filtering in. At that moment, I tried so hard not to be disappointed — in him, or myself, or all the years that had brought us here. Of course, I thought. Of course he would leave. So would I, given the chance. I would take that plane ticket and travel far enough away that the present would obliterate everything I knew.

That night, my mother called from work. "Do you know?" she asked.

"I came home and he was already gone."

I heard a piece of paper shifting, my mother adjusting the phone in her hands. "Your father called me from the airport."

I waited.

"So he's gone back." She paused, a break in her voice.

The moment hit me hard. I took a breath and then I told her, "He was miserable. I'd rather he was gone than miserable."

"Would you?" She didn't speak for a moment then she cleared her throat. "I don't blame you for thinking that. I suppose, in the end, I'll feel the same." We spoke for a few moments more and then she said, "I'll be home soon." We hung up the phone.

Later on, we found out that my father had taken care of everything. He had sold his car. He had moved the credit cards and bills to his name, so that when he declared bankruptcy for the second time, which he did just before he left, he would not drag my mother down with him. He had done all these things in consideration and politeness, but he had neglected to leave her a note. My father left her only the quiet of his departure. He must have known she would just let him go. She was never the type to follow, to beg him back.

That night, I climbed down the fire escape, let my body hang for a moment before letting go. I went next door to the IGA parking lot, where the neon lights lit the concrete pink and yellow. Turning south on Victoria Drive, I walked from streetlamp to streetlamp. On an upstairs balcony, two men sat playing cards, their voices drifting down. "That's the last I heard."

The sound of the cards shuffling. "Up in smoke." I walked until the wind and the distance exhausted me, then turned around and headed home again.

In front of our apartment, I lost my strength and sat down in the cold grass. I thought of my father standing in the doorway that night, one unspoken conversation. As if I could have changed the outcome with some small, simple act. If there were words that could have kept him here, if I had been the kind of daughter who would say them.

In some ways, leaving was my father's bravest act. He threw caution to the wind. The country that loomed so large in his imagination finally drew him back. Despite family, despite our hold on him, in the end, that place won out.

¤

When I met Will, he was thirty-one years old. There were whole lives behind us both. With him, I hoped, at first, to become someone changed. The kind of person who lives with only the present in mind, who knows in her heart that no failures, however great, are immovable. When Will first asked me to marry him, I was exuberant. I said, "I'm so happy, I want to jump out this window." He smiled and said, "Don't."

For three weeks one summer, we thought I was pregnant. I was twenty-three years old. One night, I nudged him awake, whispered, "Maybe we need counseling," and he rolled over to face me, hands on my stomach, our breaths held. "Maybe there's been some kind of mistake."

Will smiled gently. "I don't think so."

"There's so much to know. I'm just not prepared."

"What are you afraid of?"

I moved my hands on his skin, then looked up at him. "That I won't be able to get the hang of it. That I'll do something wrong."

"I'm scared too."

"But you wanted this, right?"

He nodded. "You say it like you didn't." The question in his look was unmistakable.

"I do want it."

"The truth?" he asked.

I didn't think, then, of the consequences of what I was saying. One more half-truth seemed so easy, when I had always been so reticent with him about what I needed. "The truth."

On a summer afternoon when the rain was pouring down in sheets, I went to the doctor complaining of back pain. "I was right," I told Will, when the results came back. "There's been a mistake." It's what the doctor told me. A kind of natural miscarriage, most common in the first trimester of pregnancy. "These things happen."

He said, "It was too good to be true."

That night we drank a bottle of wine, followed in quick succession by several more. Afterwards, giddy, we took the motorcycle out and raced to the university, me holding on to Will's chest. When we leaned into a curve it was pure joy. I closed my eyes, tuned to the rush of oncoming traffic, the air shattering. For the first time since I left home, I felt loose and uncontrolled. I pushed my weight back on the motorcycle, releasing my grip from Will's chest, speed tumbling through my body. Will's face, glancing back, alarmed.

That night, all our clothes left on the floor, I sat up in bed, unable to breathe. Will put his mouth to my sternum, calming me, as if he could catch the words I refused to say. And what words were they? *Stop. Go back.* I put my hands to his chest, pressured him gently away from me. Then I stood and walked out of the bedroom. Moonlight flooded our apartment, settling over everything like varnish. The furniture, distant as objects in a rear-view mirror; with each passing moment, they seemed farther behind me.

Once, walking along the suspension bridge in Lynn Canyon, I froze and couldn't move. Will stood beside me, hand on my back. "Try running all the way to the other side, without stopping," he said. "You can do it, if you don't stop to think." He went to demonstrate. My husband sprinting across Lynn

Canyon, scattering children and tourists. The bridge swaying like a high-wire rope. His body safe on the other side, chest heaving, looking back for me.

¤

When my parents left Indonesia, they walked away from a familiar life, but one foreign to all I know. Some years ago, the students in Jakarta took to the streets, protesting the government. Had my family remained there, would I have been among those students, one more in that sea of faces? Or those nights when rioters set the Chinese shophouses on fire, that bitter violence, what might have become of us then? I did not know where we fit in, or on which side of the line we might have lived.

That country lay like a stone between my parents. Once here, my mother did not look back. She worked herself to the bone but set her sights on the future. But my father could not see so far ahead. He held on to those old photographs of Indonesia, and when he pulled them out, he examined them with an appraising eye. As if to see whether the photographs were true to the memory he carried, if a picture could ever do his country justice.

The bad luck of his life was not, as he thought, a lack of opportunity or ingenuity. It was the tragedy of place. To always be in the wrong country at the wrong time, the home that needs you less than you need it.

After my father left, my mother and I moved out of the apartment in East Vancouver. We spent a month packing, emptying closets and drawers, sorting through forgotten belongings. One night, she showed me the photographs she had found in my father's desk — my parents, young and serious, in a formal portrait; their old house, lifted up on stilts. My father no longer needed to carry these, I thought. I looked at the plantations and wide skies, their unfamiliar beauty.

I set the photographs down. "Do you miss him?"

My mother touched her face, as if feeling for some emotion. "I suppose so. But what good is it? That won't change anything."

That year, there was unrest in Indonesia. Small pockets of violence erupting, then brutally dealt with by the military. I saw clips of it on the news, a few seconds, a tiny window. The Irianese were still organized, still fighting Indonesian occupation though it seemed like no one noticed. I thought of Indonesia as the place of tumult, of unrest, where a military dictatorship muscled these disparate islands together, no matter the cost. For my parents, though, no other country will ever do. Even my mother, so at home here, thinks back to those humid nights, that once-spoken language.

After we finished packing that evening, my mother fell asleep on the couch. I haunted the bedrooms, the stacks of half-full boxes, stopping for a moment to watch my mother, her chest lifting up and down, her graying hair spread out against the cushions. For the first time I pitied my father. He had gone away from us and perhaps we would not let him come back again.

From Java, Irian Jaya, then back through Sumatra, my father sent me postcards. I marked his progress through those vivid pictures, the water buffalo and *padi* fields. Once, he asked my mother to wire money to him, and she obliged. We could not guess his circumstances in those years and he did not confide in us.

One Sunday morning, four years after he had gone, my father called and said, "I'm home."

"In Jayapura?" I asked.

He paused for a moment. "No, no. Here. Vancouver."

"Where are you exactly?"

My father laughed, as if this was the question he'd been waiting for. "I've got my own bachelor suite," he said. "I'm a new man."

By that time, I was living on my own. I called my mother to give her the news. "He's back, is he?" she said. "Living in some hotel, I suppose."

"He has an apartment."

"Is that right? Well. That's a good sign."

I went across town to see him. His apartment building, near Commercial Drive, stood out, gray and rectangular. I hesitated outside. From the sidewalk, I thought I glimpsed him — this elderly man in jogging pants and a sweatshirt, standing at a fourth-floor window. He was looking out to the shipyards, the tankers on the water, the rooftops muted of color.

When my father opened the door, he was wrapped in sweaters. Vancouver was taking the bloom from his tropical tan but he looked relaxed. "You're here," he said, smiling broadly.

I smiled back, trying to feel at ease. "I'm here."

We embraced very briefly, and I noticed then how thin he had become. He had aged, and his face was dark and lined. Standing in the entrance, I could see the entire apartment. It was small, a kitchen and a living room in one. My father ushered me inside. He gave me the tour, laughing as he did so, saying, "I'm living the bachelor life now. I don't need much more than this." I glanced at his furniture — a table, a mattress, and one plastic chair.

He busied himself at the stove, disappearing behind the steam. The air in the apartment was rich with the smell of spices, ginger, lemon grass, hot pepper. "*Chilli kepeting,*" he called to me, over the sound of the food frying. "I remember how much you liked this."

Up in the corners, the walls were moldy and gray and the carpets had a lingering scent, part cigarettes, part damp. He'd done the best he could with decorations. There were Christmas cards, hung up along a line of string, and certificates from the real estate office framed on the wall. *For Devoted Service. For Congeniality.* I walked onto his tiny balcony, looked across the road at the ramshackle apartments, the wet leaves running bright along the gutters. Out on the harbor, two yellow sulphur hills glowed neon against the clouded sky.

"It's ready then," my father said, setting lunch down on the table. There was only one chair so my father sat on his mattress, plate balanced on his lap. He looked me up and down. "Eat," he said, smiling happily.

Through the walls, I could hear the shadow of a conversation, interrupted by the play-by-play of a ball game. At one point, my father asked me, "How is your mother?"

"She's fine. She's been working hard, as usual."

He nodded, face lifting up. "Does she want to see me at all?"

I shook my head. My mother had prepared me for this question before I came. "I don't think so," I told him, as gently as I could. "Not right away."

My father looked at me, his expression bewildered.

We ate in silence for a few moments. Then I asked him, "Will you be going back to real estate?"

He glanced at me searchingly, then dropped his gaze. "I don't know."

"But what will you do for money?"

My father didn't answer. He moved on to a different topic, the cold weather, the early winter. I noticed how the cuffs of his sweater were frayed and his hands were those of an old man, wiry and marked by liver spots. After we had finished lunch and he was clearing the dishes, he said, "I managed to borrow money while I was away. But it ran out while I was in Indonesia." He turned the tap on, moving the dishes underneath. "I'm on welfare, but don't worry about me. It's only for the time being."

We went outside and stood together on the balcony, and I told my father that I was planning to marry. He looked out at the grid of streets running down to the docks and said, "So soon?"

It made me smile, because I knew he still thought of me as a young girl. I laughed. "Don't worry. I'm sure you'll like him."

My father seemed to consider this. Then he smiled at me. "It's good that you found someone. It isn't necessary to be alone."

Afterwards, when I stood up to leave, he walked me to the door. He waited there, as if he could not step over the line that would separate him from where he now lived. One hand gripped the door frame, the knuckles white.

I leaned towards him and kissed his cheek. "I'll call." Then I ducked out into the hallway, down the elevator to the ground floor. Outside, I couldn't see straight, the rain was coming down so hard. On Commercial Drive, a man and his two Labradors sat on the sidewalk. He held his hands out to me, asking for spare change, but I hurried by, anxious to be gone. So this was the result, I thought, of being brave. Of dismantling your life. I walked away from my father's apartment, under the rain cascading off the awnings, past the barred-up storefronts. No emotion came to me, though I walked across the city that afternoon, kept walking until my body could go no more.

¤

Will used to say that happiness is something you just take. It's sitting there like a package in a store and you either pick it up or walk by. I told him nothing was that simple. Sometimes circumstances colluded against a person. It's a nose-dive, I told him, and you can't pull out of it.

"Some people choose unhappiness," Will said.

"Sometimes unhappiness chooses them."

"Like your father."

"Will, we've been through this before."

"At some point, you're going to have to deal with this. You can't pretend he doesn't exist."

"This is not something I want to talk about with you."

"Then what is? What do you think we should be talking about?" He put both hands to his temples and shook his head.

By that time, I had not been to see my father in almost a year. But this failing of mine was private. The grief I felt was not open to discussion. When Will tried to talk about it, I shut down, turned and left.

Now and then, it disappeared. All that tension evaporated and we could approach each other again, though tentatively. I lay in bed, Will's entire body flat on top of mine like a wrestling move to pin me down. Will looked at me with an expression I thought was long gone. Amazement, wonder. But underneath his expression there was sadness. "Don't worry so much," he said. "We'll get through this."

He put his hand to my stomach, traced a line from left to right as if he could see that tension and he could track it down.

The night that we learned that the pregnancy was over, I finally felt released. Removed, suddenly, from the course I had set out on. I leaned back on the motorcycle then, arms dropping, and Will put one hand to my thigh, as if that could hold me there. He kept going, along a curved road overlooking the cliffs. He was the kind of person who would love me despite all my failings. But I could not continue. That image of my father remained with me, his one suitcase, his solitary self crossing the ocean in search of things remembered. A backwards journey to remake the future.

Living alone and on social assistance, my father's condition did not improve. During my infrequent visits, on my way to somewhere else, I noticed that the walls were slowly emptying. The Christmas cards came down first. Then the plaques. There were pills lined up on the kitchen counter, an arsenal against depression and loneliness. My father put on weight and lost it, put on weight and lost it. Once or twice, late at night, he had called my mother, hoping to go back. She had let him down gently. When he confided this to me, I could only nod, unsure what response I could give.

How could I change his circumstances? I didn't know and so I chose to withdraw. There were emotions that he carried — disappointment, regret — that I wanted gone from my present life, as if they had everything to do with him and they had no root in me. My father saw my reluctance and accepted it, as if it was all he could rightly ask for. He did not demand more.

During our visits, he always reached for his photo album. When he bowed his head, I could see how thin his neck looked, how precarious. That air of resignation that he carried was still palpable, it filled the room.

We would start at the beginning. My father as a boy, standing in short pants at someone's wedding. Then at twenty-five, my age now, leaning against a tree, his face full of pride. He had a picture of us from years ago, blue mountains in the backdrop, but only my father is staring straight ahead, into the camera. My mother and I are distracted, drawn to invisible points to the left or right. When we came to a picture of my mother, alone, my father always paused to examine her. He half-covered the photo with one hand, as if he could only manage a piece of her at a time, now her dress, now her arms, now her face.

One night in September, Will and I fell into our old habit. He brought out both the helmets and we climbed onto the motorcycle.

He took us out to West Vancouver, where the highway is cut into the cliffs, precarious above the ocean. The road curved dramatically and Will leaned far to the side, wind rushing on the downhill slope. Over the city skyline, the sun was lowering and the moon was full; neither day nor night. Those thin skyscrapers seemed to float on the water. In all the newspaper boxes along the way, there were pictures of Indonesia, flags flying in Timor, a referendum, finally, to decide the future.

At a lookout, Will leaned the bike onto a shoulder. We got down, pulling our helmets off. There were islands in the water, bare trees sharp on the surface. Will pointed out the nearest one. "That's Bowen, isn't it? Didn't we camp there years ago?"

"I think so. I can hardly remember now."

Will looked out, nodding. "It rained," he said, his breath clouding the air. "I remember that it rained the whole time."

He stood up and walked to the edge of the lookout, pointed out the other islands, their strange, heavy shapes. I watched his glance moving over the ocean. "You're barely here," he said, turning.

I reached my hand out to touch his face. But his expression was so open and so trusting, it made me hesitate. "I didn't expect this."

He looked at me questioningly.

"Perhaps I never knew what I wanted." Will's whole body seemed to sag but I continued on. "I mistakenly thought I wanted this. And I don't. I know that now."

"Miriam," Will said.

"This isn't what I want," I said. "I'm sorry."

"Explain it."

I shook my head. I didn't know any more if I even loved him, or what I had once believed. Will's expression was beseeching. He deserved an explanation from me, but I could feel my emotions shutting off, clean and hard. "I'm sorry," I said. "I can't."

Will looked at me for a long moment. "Forgive me," he said, when he finally spoke. "But it's cowardly. This is a cowardly act."

"Don't tell me that."

"You're walking away with as little resistance as possible. You think this will save you somehow. From what, I don't know."

"I'm just trying to do what's best."

"What's best? You don't even know that. You can't even be bothered to figure out what that would be." He shook his head, impatient. "It angers me, how little you're willing to risk for me and for yourself."

It had started to rain and Will pulled his hood up. The water fell forward in front of his eyes in a thin waterfall. All I had to do was lift my hands and grab hold, but I refused. How could I tell him that I did not understand it myself? Whatever feeling was necessary, whatever energy I needed, seemed gone. He was right, I wanted it all to disappear.

Later, when we climbed back onto the bike, I put my arms around his chest, hands flat. The bike took off and I watched the highway. The line of a mountain range ran alongside us, an unbroken, hazy shadow, a separate history, a different life.

Will booked a ticket home to Ontario to give us some time apart. After he had left, I tried to picture him there — exhaling drifts of air, man in the snow. Walking, he sinks a few inches down. He's very cold and the expression on his face is stoic. At home, I lost myself in wild thoughts. Catching my face in the mirror, I was surprised by my expression — stunned. Uncertain. Cut loose from what I knew.

Once, Will and I stood in my father's apartment and tried to find all the ways that the map of the world had changed. The Soviet Union was the most dramatic. The country crumbling at the edges — Estonia, Latvia, then falling away like a landslide. We stared at the map in wonder. My father knew Southeast Asia. Will knew the ancient cultures of art, the old foundations — Mesopotamia, Byzantine — that once existed. I loved Vancouver, the city wading out into the ocean, the border of mountains. There we are in my memory, each of us drawn to a different region, each of us straying our hands across a different country.

In the days after Will left, I turned that picture of us over again and again in my mind. At that time, the news was filled with Indonesia. In East Timor, the region had exploded in violence. There were photographs of refugees, the widespread displacement. I stood at my kitchen table, turning the pages of the newspaper, unsure then whom I was, in fact, grieving for. I recognized my own selfishness. When I saw those pictures, I ached for the country I had never seen, the parts of Will and my family I had never recognized, the loss that seemed so unresolvable.

When I was younger, I used to study all the details of Indonesia, its wealth and beauty, its lost ages. As if I could understand my father and myself by knowing this, as if what I needed could be compiled, written down, and it would shore me up against the present day.

¤

Two weeks after Will went back to Ontario, the first snowfall of the year took the city by surprise. I lay in bed listening to the phone ringing. It must be Will, I thought, but I did not know what to say to him. Lying in bed, I could see rooftops. The snowfall had cloaked the landscape, so that now it seemed a place where you could walk for days with no sense of moving forward.

I remembered the time I was a child, when I came down with pneumonia. My father blamed the snow. We had tobogganed on Mount Seymour, sliding on Glad bags down the hill. Late at night, my father bundled me up and we drove home, down the dark mountainside, the quiet roads where only a handful of cars slipped and skidded on the ice. The radio warned us to "Stay in if you can. If you can't drive in the snow, don't." My father drove with both hands gripping the wheel, squeezed the brake worriedly. The sky was luminescent with stars.

By morning, I was feverish and hallucinating. My father was already at work, turning the *Closed* sign over, polishing the glass, dusting the gleaming wood of the French Provincial sofas. My mother and I caught a bus to the hospital. In the late afternoon, my father came and drove us home. I was bundled into the back seat. Through the windows I could watch the city blur by — tops of trees, neon signs. The car was warm and self-contained, a moving house.

In the front seat, my parents spoke in whispered voices. "Noo-moan-ya," my father said, testing the word out.

At home, my father fed me rice porridge from a plastic spoon. In the hollow of the spoon was a picture of two boys playing soccer. They became part of my dream state. I thought I was speaking to my father. I was telling him how the boys were running ahead and I was so far behind them, but my father was holding out a blue bicycle. He was running beside me, pushing me off on my blue bike. Out I went, twirling like an acrobat, into the wide world. My father nodded and smiled, his hand cooling my forehead.

On a cold, windy day when I felt stronger, we took a walk through the tree-lined streets, beside the drifts of snowbanks. My father cut an icicle down and presented it to me and I held it gingerly in my mittened hands. "You have to take care of yourself," he said sternly. He was always concerned about my well-being.

I nodded, comforted by his attentions.

"Don't strain yourself or get upset."

"I won't."

"Good girl." He patted my hair. "One day you will buy me a very large house."

After the sun went down that afternoon, I sat at my bedroom window. In the backyard, my father was building a snowman. My mother took a photograph, white flash in the dark, of my father standing beside his creation, one arm wrapped around its snowy body. Inside, the image, ghostly, stayed with me. My father in the snow, smiling for all the world to see.

The phone rang all morning but no one left a message. I wandered from room to room in the apartment, picking things up at random, then putting them down. Will's books were still stacked in pyramids on the floor. *Art in the Byzantine Era, Rubens to Picasso,* and, at the very bottom, *What to Expect: The Toddler Years.* I flipped through, laughing at Will's notes in the margins. He must have gone through and underlined the art references: "Food blowing. Certain foods lend themselves better to dramatic expulsion." And: "To some toddlers, a bowel movement is a remarkable personal statement, a crowning achievement, something to celebrate, revel in, and if the spirit so moves them, decorate with." In the margin, Will had sketched a big-headed baby, with a list of names underneath: *Dumbo. Tin Tin. Babe. Hey Yu.*

I turned the radio on but all they could talk about was the weather. This city, with its temperate climate, was always struck dumb by snow. Buses were grounded, the roads undriveable. I rummaged through the fridge, found an old frozen pizza, and set it in the oven. Then, pulling a jacket on, I walked outside. The kids next door stumbled through the white, diving head first into snowbanks. They pelted each other with snowballs. Beside them, an elderly man shoveled his driveway. He tipped his fragile body forward, his breath unfurling into the thin, blue air.

What would Will say if he were here? He'd say, "This is packing snow, all right," both arms stretched out, a wide smile. "Ontario packing snow." When I lifted my face to the sky, the snow headed straight for me, converging between my eyes.

Inside, while I shook the powder from my shoes, the phone started up again.

"Thank God," my mother said, before I'd even said hello. "Thank God you're home."

A car outside the window stole my attention. It fishtailed left, slow motion, then burrowed into a snowbank.

"Miriam, I'm so sorry. Something's happened."

The passenger door of the stalled car popped open. The driver climbed out and stood still, watching the snow come down.

"Miriam? Are you there?"

"I'm here."

"Your father," she said. "Someone found him."

The room was moving. I couldn't concentrate. Outside, the driver of the car was walking away. "What happened?"

"I'm sorry. I'm so sorry." Her voice broke. Then, "Miriam, you need to get here now. We're at Vancouver General. Your father attempted suicide."

I looked around the room. "I can't."

"Why not?"

"There's something in the oven," I said, my voice rising higher. "I can't come right now."

"Miriam, listen. The buses are stopped. There are no cars on the road. I couldn't get hold of you. You need to come right now, okay? Do you understand?"

She hung up first. I stared out the window, at the car abandoned in the road. An inch of snow coating the roof.

I was still wearing my coat. When I opened the oven door, the pizza was still there, wrapped in plastic, frozen solid. The oven was cold. This made me laugh, an unsettling sound that filled the room then stopped, broken off. Somehow, I knelt down on the floor and put my shoes back on. I turned all the lights off, then let myself out the front door. The walk to the hospital wasn't long, perhaps fifteen minutes, but I wondered if it was possible that I was too late. Not only in body, but in desire, in thought. And if not too late, then something else. Too blind.

Through the snowfall, I could see the red Emergency lights. I walked through the automatic doors to the reception desk and gave my father's name. A nurse pointed me upstairs. Somebody took my hand, another nurse, and we turned off the main hallway, pushed our way through a set of double doors, into a very silent corridor. She opened a door to the waiting room, off to the side, and led me through.

"You're here," my mother said, looking up. She came and embraced me, her warm hands against my face. "You're freezing."

"Is it too late?"

She put both hands on my shoulders. I bent my head towards her until my forehead was resting against her chest. "You made it," she said, very gently. "It's okay."

Her eyes were red and tired. She took my coat and then together we walked to Intensive Care. A doctor joined us and he started speaking very softly. Then we stepped behind a white curtain and I looked away, up to the ceiling. When I looked down, I could see the machine that monitored my father's breathing. His heartbeat was amplified in the room, the sound like a slow dance, open and even, open and slow. There was a metal pole, silver hooks to hold an intravenous bag. A deep cut ran along his forehead, partially bandaged. They had fastened an oxygen mask to his mouth.

Eyes closed, my father swiped clumsily at the mask, trying to dislodge it. His hand missed, then grazed it, moving the mask slightly to the left. He swiped once more, hitting the tube in his throat. I grabbed his hand and held on; it seemed very small and light. His eyes stayed shut.

"It's me," I said. His hand felt loose and full of bones, not at all like what I remembered. My father opened his eyes and looked at me. He breathed my name. I wept, then. I couldn't stop it.

That minute, standing beside him, seemed to last forever. I was holding on to my father when the doctor came to re-adjust the mask. "He fell," someone said.

I nodded and then I pulled away. My father's grip grew tighter. I brought my other hand to rest on his and I removed his hand, as gently as I could, until both hands were free. Behind me, someone lowered the blinds. A nurse came and unhooked an intravenous bag. I pushed through the curtain blindly. My mother's hands were on my shoulders. "Miriam," she said, but I was already walking away down the wide hallway, through the double doors, walking until they let me go, through the maze of hallways and stair- cases, following one colored line then another, as if to lose them. Past white walls and reception islands, nurses moving and laughing and watching. Will, I thought. If only Will were here. I felt my way outside, blind now, into the cold afternoon. The snow was dropping fast. I stood still, one of my arms reaching out to catch it, swimming in front of my eyes as if it had come loose.

I remember my father had a calendar on the wall in his apartment. He used to cross each day off, one by one, as if counting towards an end point. For me the years were indistinguishable, unbordered pieces of time. But he was never blessed with such forgetful- ness. Pills and alcohol, my mother told me. Until he lost consciousness and fell, cutting his forehead. He was on the floor eleven hours before someone found him. They had heard his voice calling from the apart- ment. The apartment manager unlocked the door. My father was dressed in a suit, like one worn for a wedding. The paramedics came. My father asked for his family, kept asking until he lost consciousness.

Inside the apartment, the walls were bare. The calendar, the map folded up and put away. The balcony door ajar, letting the cold into the room.

We stayed with him all night. Through the glass windows, I could see the snow falling. It wiped the landscape clean. It seemed that only we existed, my mother, my father, and me, as it had been on those long drives across the city, the miles we covered. The hospital staff walked in and out, passing through the periphery like figments of my imagination; only the three of us in the center.

My father's body was thin beneath the blankets. The skin on his neck fell in loose folds. Once, he used to be so careful, dyeing the gray from his hair. Now his hair had gone completely white, that coat of color disappeared.

From time to time, he opened his eyes and regarded us as if from a great distance. Then my mother would take his hand, she would stroke his brow. It was the same as before, I thought. Where he was going, into another country or into another life, I could not follow. Yet when he opened his eyes I knew he was looking back for us. His eyes were no longer guarded and neither were ours. They said only the most essential words. *No. Not like this.* And the fear and doubt that I had hoarded and kept near, I finally saw them for what they were. Nothing at all. The aftermath of memory.

The intimacy of seeing his body in the bed, of listening to each private breath. His hands, loose and open. My mother beside me, one hand on the small of my back.

Throughout that week, my father remained in critical condition. We kept a vigil, my mother rising and standing beside him, then I would take my turn. We kept our silence, as we always had, but this one was different. It was not filled with the unspoken. We simply existed in this tiny room, the lights dim. My father's vital signs like handwriting, moving across a black screen.

When the sun rose on the fourth day, my mother walked me to the hospital entrance. "You need to sleep," she told me, touching my forehead. "This is the long haul."

Outside, she looked at the empty road. "He loves you," she said. "He's always had such dreams for you. I'm sorry." She stopped, seeing my expression. "I'm not saying it to hurt you. I just want you to understand. You never could have disappointed him." She looked away.

I watched her turn back to the Emergency entrance, the doors parting to let her through. Then I walked through the parking lot, past the ambulances lined up and waiting.

A thick fog had settled over the skyline. It wiped the sky clear of mountains and water. I walked along Broadway, past Main Street, where paper cups and newspapers littered the sidewalk. Past the sign that, years ago, my father told me was the tallest free-standing sign in the world. "There it is," my father said proudly. "Bowmac. Biggest sign in the world." He also showed me the narrowest building that still stands in Chinatown. My father, the tour guide who took me everywhere. He must have loved this city. Now it was coated with snow. A white-out, everything vanished, as if this were a game, as if I could bring it back from memory.

At home, I unlocked my apartment and turned all the lights on. The message light was flashing, a slow red like a heartbeat, a siren.

My mother's voice. "He's resting comfortably. They say we might be through the worst."

I stood listening to the message play itself out. The tape ended. My warm, empty apartment with all the lights blazing, my sadness like another body beside me, making me unsure, making me weep. If I could lay it all out, every detail, every gesture, would I come to peace with it, and then myself?

Will would say, look at it differently. Turn it all upside down. Say that we let each other go as a gesture of love.

I called Will from a pay phone outside the hospital. Feeding quarters into the slot every few moments because I could not stop speaking.

I told him that it used to be that I would wake thinking of my father, his life as it was then, him alone in his apartment, living from hand to mouth. I would think of him and yet I could not bring myself to go to him.

I can see now how my father and I were the same. Waiting until the breaking point. Then, for him, pills and alcohol one night, an act that made all the words fall silent.

"I'll be home soon," Will said.

Even now I go back, holding the details up to my eyes, magnifying the tiny pieces to find the one that speaks volumes. In the end, this must only be for me, my selfish love. Packing and unpacking it, to see if something different comes to the surface. I want to know because there's hope now, and I do not want to make the same mistakes again.

When my father became conscious finally, he was frightened. "You must leave now," he mumbled.

"Hurry. Call the police." A side effect, the doctor told me. The drugs were making him fearful. When I stood at his bedside, he grasped my hand, said, "Did you call the police?" and I said, "Yes."

Anything seemed possible. The walls were shifting, straight and curved like an Escher print. My father lost himself in wild imaginings that none of us were privy to. My father said, "There's been a mistake."

"Yes," I told him. "I'll straighten it out."

He muttered in Indonesian, *Apakah anda pasti?* and I answered, "No, I am not certain at all."

In the nights that followed, I slept on a chair beside my father's bed. I woke up to the night sky, its flood of stars, and remembered the three of us traversing the empty roads on our Sunday drives. Those tunnels and arteries. It used to be that we could lose ourselves in them, before we came to know the city well.

Each morning, my mother arrived with a cup of coffee in one hand, the newspaper in the other. She took the chair that I vacated, and read to my father for a short while. Slowly, my father came back to the world, his eyes open and full. I watched, from outside the room, knowing this moment would pass. But I drank it in, to see them side by side.

¤

Last Sunday, I drove out to Hastings Street and the neighborhood where I grew up. I looked for the old store, but the glass storefronts had changed too much. I had thought that what was so vivid in my imagination would call out to me in real life, as if in verification. Will, in the passenger seat, said perhaps the building had been torn down long ago. To make way for something else, a different building, a new development. He was right, I knew, but still I thought I should recognize the place.

We got out of the car and walked along the sidewalk. It was fall, and the leaves had come down. The branches were stark and lovely. Near to us, on the sidewalk, a little boy in a blue raincoat ran headlong through the crowd of people. We could not see where he was headed, only that his arms were stretched out to both sides, like an airplane. I thought that someone would eventually catch him, his feet swinging off the ground, and lift him high. They would give him an aerial view of this street, these stores, all the people crowding along. On the hill, the cars struggled up the incline, halting and nervous, and the streetlamps began to burn. The little boy disappeared ahead of us, into the crowd. I knew, then, that I would not find it. But still I walked in the direction he had gone, at home in this place, though every landmark had disappeared.

ACKNOWLEDGMENTS

Some of these stories first appeared as follows: "Alchemy" in the *Malahat Review;* "Four Days from Oregon" in the *Fiddlehead* and *99: Best Canadian Stories;* "House" in the *Fiddlehead;* and "Simple Recipes" in *Event* and *The Journey Prize Anthology 10.*

I gratefully acknowledge the editors, especially Calvin Wharton, Ross Leckie, and Denise Ryan, who published these and other stories in earlier forms, and whose support has been invaluable.

My deepest thanks to Rick Maddocks, for his patience and encouragement beyond all measure; and to Amanda Okopski and Dean Bakopoulos, for a friendship that has spanned many years and many countries. And to Willem, all my love.

Thanks to the Department of Creative Writing at the University of British Columbia for their many kindnesses. I am indebted to Asya Muchnick at Little, Brown, and Marilyn Biderman and Kelly Hyatt at McClelland & Stewart, for their encouragement and unfailing commitment. And finally, to my editor at M&S, Ellen Seligman — all my gratitude and admiration.

About the Author

Madeleine Thien is the Canadian-born daughter of Malaysian-Chinese immigrants. She holds an MFA in creative writing from the University of British Columbia. *Simple Recipes*, her first book, was selected as a notable book by the Kiriyama Pacific Rim Prize in 2001. She is also the recipient of a City of Vancouver Award, a Canadian Authors Association Air Canada Award, and an Asian Canadian Writers Workshop Emerging Writer Award for fiction. She lives in Vancouver, British Columbia.

simple

recipes

Stories by Madeleine Thien

A Reading Group Guide

A Conversation with
the Author of *Simple Recipes*

Madeleine Thien talks with Kathleen Walker
of www.FictionAddiction.net

Where does your inspiration originate?
It usually happens that I start with an image. In "House," I had
this idea of two girls sitting on the grass, waiting over the course
of a day. People pass by them, but they just sit and wait.

I wrote this story around this idea, trying to understand
where this enormous patience might come from. After a while,
I started to think that they believed that by staying still, by
having faith, they could bring back some part of the past.

Who are the greatest influences on your writing?
Up until now, the greatest influences on my writing have been
Alice Munro, Michael Ondaatje, and Michael Ignatieff. There's
something about the kind of stories they choose to tell and
how they tell them — it reminds me that fiction can be trans-
formative. It can change the way we view ourselves and the
world around us. I'm also a great admirer of Gabriel García
Márquez, Chang-rae Lee, and Anne Michaels.

**In a number of your stories the main characters are children.
Why?**
I think there was something about the way children interact
with the world that I wanted to express. The children, or ado-

lescents, are confronting the complexity of their experiences, trying to make sense of them. Despite their powerlessness, they are also trying to find a way to act with dignity, despite their young age.

I remember, as a child, having a lot of time to think and to question, and to wonder and tease out the meaning in sometimes incomprehensible experiences. Maybe, as adults, we forget to do that sometimes. We think we already know how the world works.

Why do you prefer working on short stories rather than a novel?
At the time, short stories felt like the right form. Something small, but whole. There were thematic questions that recurred in my writing, and I wanted to put these in a form where there was tension, because that allowed for different ideas and possible answers to come to the surface.

What do you want people to take away from your stories?
That's a good question and a hard one, too. For me, the characters in these stories experience some very difficult things. It's how they incorporate those experiences into their lives, and into their sense of who they are as individuals, that is important to me. Somehow their experiences lead them to recognize the complexity of themselves and of other people.

There's a line that has stuck in my head from Susan Griffin's *A Chorus of Stones*, "How much do we know or not know in those we love?" The characters are attempting to know and understand the experiences and the people around them as fully as they know themselves. Maybe this is impossible, but I think the attempt is necessary.

The majority of your short stories in this book deal with the parent-child relationship. Does this come from your relationship with your parents?

Maybe. I'm sure my relationship with my parents has influenced the book. Not in an autobiographical way exactly. More that I'm part of my parents, and also wholly separate from them, and that idea of simultaneous nearness and distance is something that interests me.

Why did you choose "Simple Recipes" as the title piece?

It sort of chose itself. It was the first story I wrote for this collection and I think a lot of the questions contained within it recur and are expanded in other stories. That story felt like a true starting point.

The underlying theme in this work seems to be a longing for the impossible. Are there any reasons for this?

Maybe that in order to change the world, you have to long for something better, something more equitable. This longing, this thinking about what we long for, might help steer us toward that kind of world.

Where do you hope your writing takes you next?

I'm working on a novel now that is set partly in British North Borneo during and after the Second World War. Memory and war have always fascinated me, and I hope with this book that I can say something true and meaningful for my generation and also the one that came before, who experienced that war and so many others.

The complete text of this interview can be found at www.FictionAddiction.net. Reprinted with permission.

Questions and Topics
for Discussion

1. Compare the relationships between the fathers and daughters depicted in the stories "Simple Recipes," "Four Days from Oregon," and "House." How are they similar and how are they different in each story?

2. In "Four Days from Oregon," Irene chooses to take her three young daughters and leave her husband to begin a life with another man. How does the narrator's view of this decision change over the course of the story? What do you think of Irene's decision and the way she carries it out?

3. The narrator of "Dispatch" does not leave her husband, even after receiving proof that he loves another woman. How do you account for her choice? How do you see their relationship evolving from the point that the story leaves off?

4. In "Alchemy," how does the narrator's view of her own sexuality develop over the course of the story? How does her relationship with her friend Paula influence it?

5. After Paula tells Miriam the truth about her father's abuse, the narrator of "Alchemy" accepts a ride home from a stranger.

She says, "I opened the passenger door and thought, this is what it all comes to" (page 71). What does she mean by this? Why does she take such a risk?

6. What role do brothers and sisters play in one another's lives in these stories? In "Simple Recipes," "Four Days from Oregon," and "House," how do the choices of the adults in their lives affect the bonds between siblings?

7. In "Bullet Train" we meet Harold and Thea both in their early lives and as adults. In what way does what we learn about their past inform the rest of the story?

8. Harold and Thea in "Bullet Train" are one of the few happy couples in this collection. What distinguishes their relationship from many of the other relationships depicted in these stories?

9. In "Bullet Train," Harold doesn't try to stop Josephine from running away, even though he thinks it's going to break her mother's heart (page 154). Why doesn't he interfere? Is he right not to?

10. In "A Map of the City," how is Miriam's marriage affected by her relationship with her parents? Why does she tell Will so little about her family?

11. At the beginning of "A Map of the City," Miriam and her father seem to be very close. Yet she reveals that "my father would often say that I had ruined his life" (page 165). How does this seeming contradiction inform their later relationship? How does Miriam's view of her father change as she grows up?

The Evidence Against Her

A novel by Robb Forman Dew

"A gorgeous, important book.... Dew's characters are fiercely imagined, fiercely alive on the page."
— Beth Kephart, *Chicago Tribune*

"At the book's end ... there is that tremendous satisfaction that only this multigenerational kind of story can give. Robb Forman Dew has a powerful way with prose. Her language is lush and beautiful." — Joanna Rose, *Portland Oregonian*

House of Women

A novel by Lynn Freed

"Irresistible.... An unusual and unusually satisfying novel."
— Kathryn Harrison, *New York Times Book Review*

"*House of Women* is surprising and inevitable, often in the same sentence. It illuminates and, at the same time, deepens the human mystery. I don't ask for more from a book."
— Michael Cunningham, author of *The Hours*

 Available wherever books are sold

The Gospel of Judas

A novel by Simon Mawer

"A superior novel. . . . A noteworthy achievement. . . . An intellectual thriller of uncommon substance."
— Chauncey Mabe, *Boston Globe*

"Mawer's prose is admirably lyrical, playful, and precise. His greatest strength, however, is in crafting probing, puzzlelike narratives that yield compelling dramas of the mind and heart."
— Michael Upchurch, *Atlantic Monthly*

Martin Sloane

A novel by Michael Redhill

"A striking first novel. . . . Reading *Martin Sloane* made me feel melancholic, hopeful, amused, energized, enlightened, unnerved, touched, and finally grateful that occasionally a writer comes along who gets real life just right."
— Bliss Broyard, *New York Times Book Review*

"A deeply moving first novel that reveals human truths with grace and humor. It is a book of constant surprises."
— Michael Ondaatje

 Available wherever books are sold

Sea Glass

A novel by Anita Shreve

"A helluva read. . . . Shreve simply has the Gift — the ability to hook you from the first page, draw you in and pull you along, and not let go until the final word."

— Zofia Smardz, *Washington Post Book World*

"Shreve's four-hankie plots are pure silk, and her characters are so real you can feel them sitting next to you on the couch."

— Michelle Vellucci, *People*

All the Finest Girls

A novel by Alexandra Styron

"An impressive, highly charged novel about a virtually taboo subject — nannying — displaying keen insight into the burdens of inheritance in its many forms: money, love, creative temperament."

— Benjamin Anastas, *New York Observer*

"Extremely moving and powerful."

— Heller McAlpin, *Washington Post Book World*